Praise for *Lights On*

"It is a great satisfaction to read this book and feel how deeply I may ponder it and find no effort lacking. All the threads are fully spun, all woven together. It is a well-made whole."

—Melinda Johnson, author of *Shepherding Sam*

"Tuggle has a wonderfully poetic voice that makes this story as deep and rich as the ancient ground beneath the characters' feet. It is a delight to the senses in the way she grounds us in the sights, sounds, and scents of the Pennsylvania mountains, and a refreshment for the spirit in the way she shows us the spiritual reality existing within and around the physical world."

—Bev Cooke, author of *Royal Monastic* and *Keeper of the Light*

"A wise and warm exploration of the bonds of farm life, faith, and the saving grace of family."

—Michael Heaton, author of the Minister of Culture column, *The Plain Dealer*

"Jess leads a quiet country life, but one interrupted by catastrophe. An early experience of the divine marks him, but he spends years learning to appreciate it, years in which those he loves, faithful and otherwise, shape his way of being in the world. Being with him is at once comfortable and challenging, but the rhythms of a farm life and the warmth of the men and women who live it, beautifully imagined, allow us a certain refreshment and even, perhaps, moments of light."

—M. Berry, Missouri State University

"*Lights on the Mountain* has no unnecessary or trite characters. All, especially Jess, are given the time needed to discover and enter into the deep peace that comes from finding the solid ground chosen for them by their Lord. Truly the sign of a good book. I was quite disappointed to reach the end."

—Rev. Mother Magdalena

"This novel glows with a quiet beauty. The characters live. The love stories transcend any romance novel I've ever read, while remaining rooted in Pennsylvania soil. Gorgeously written, the very turns of phrase help readers see the world in new ways. Tuggle may well have birthed a new genre, a decidedly American Eastern Orthodox literary fiction."

—Leslie Baynes, Associate Professor of New Testament, Missouri State University

"Like a Russian nesting doll, except every layer is richer, the deeper you go. Gorgeous prose, complicated characterization, and a barely evident sense of provident grace combine to make this a book that forces you to stop, listen to the silences between words, and glory in the beauty hidden there. A book to return to again and again."

—Nicholas Kotar, author of *The Song of the Sirin* and the *Raven Son* series

LIGHTS ON THE MOUNTAIN

A NOVEL

CHERYL ANNE TUGGLE

PARACLETE
FICTION

2019 First Printing
Lights on the Mountain:
A Novel

ISBN 978-1-64060-166-6

Paraclete Fiction is an imprint of Paraclete Press, Inc., the Paraclete Fiction name and logo (wing) are trademarks of Paraclete Press, Inc.

Lights on the Mountain is a work of fiction. All names, characters, places, and incidents are either a product of the author's imagination or are used fictitiously, and any resemblance to actual persons, establishments, events, or locales is entirely coincidental.

Library of Congress Cataloging-in-Publication Data
Names: Tuggle, Cheryl Anne, 1964- author.
Title: Lights on the mountain : a novel / Cheryl Anne Tuggle.
Description: Brewster, Massachusetts : Paraclete Press, 2018.
Identifiers: LCCN 2018031179 | ISBN 9781640601666 (paperback)
Subjects: | BISAC: RELIGION / Christianity / Literature & the Arts. | FICTION / Christian / General. | FICTION / Religious. | GSAFD: Christian fiction
Classification: LCC PS3620.U375 L54 2018 | DDC 813.6/—dc23
LC record available at https://lccn.loc.gov/2018031179

10 9 8 7 6 5 4 3 2 1

Published by Paraclete Press | Brewster, Massachusetts | www.paracletepress.com
Printed in the United States of America

Get thee out of thy country,
and from thy kindred,
and from thy father's house,
unto a land that I will show thee.
—Genesis 12:1 (KJV)

Dawn and resurrection are synonymous.
—Victor Hugo

To earth hast Thou come down O Master, to save Adam;
and not finding him on earth, Thou hast descended into hell,
seeking him there.
—Lamentations of Holy Saturday

For my husband, who is proof that a good man is not so very hard to find

and

to the nuns

IT WAS FOREORDAINED. That's what Gracie's mama would claim when all that was to take place had taken place. And though Darya Morozov was a religious woman, sure of many things Jess Hazel considered too uncertain to be certain, there were times. Maybe a beam of October sun would come slipping through the window and set Galina's hair on fire. Or David Busco would go limping home from Muddy Creek in a red blaze of dusk, fish basket heavy with trout. Times when Jess would remember Kerry Mountain transfigured at dawn, a lesser Sinai of the Allegheny Plateau, and be obliged to admit that Gracie's mama might be right. There was, after all, no proof she wasn't.

Perhaps it all was in some unfathomable way meant to happen as it did. For as Darya put it: How else does the tall, tall man with the sober jaw and the eyes planted so deep find the girl who can see the promise of harvest in them? Unless she believes, as Gracie did, that farmers may also be saints and mountain-dwelling fools, holy.

CONTENTS

PART ONE

1

Hazel Valley
Prospect, Pennsylvania
May 1, 1952
5:53 AM

When Jess Hazel left the warmth of the house that morning of the Light and trudged down the hill to the barn, he did it with unusual reluctance. He was in a dark mood, tired to the bone after another long night of poor sleep. The conversation between his parents, low and tense and punctuated by his mother's sobs, had gone so late it was early by the time it ended. How early, he did not know. If he had risen to check the time, Clyde and Millie would have known he was lying awake in the room above theirs, every nerve stretched tight. What he did know was that by 5:30, when he'd left his bed unrested, all sound had ceased. And he knew that down in the kitchen, the percolator, which should have been working at a pot of coffee strong enough to get him through chores, was as cold and silent as the house. Seeing it, he had crept back upstairs to finish dressing in the dark, cursing the bed across from his own. Cursing the absence of his only brother in it.

The Fourth of July would mark a year since Walter had up and joined the Marines, got himself shipped off to Parris Island for basic training and from there to Korea, to help solve that peck of trouble. Jess missed him with the pain of a phantom limb. Two years and three months between them, but he and Walter were as close as twins. So close, they were, in fact, that Jess sometimes pondered, as he was inclined to do all life's hidden things, the strength of their bond. A pure gift, he would most often decide, after considering awhile. What else could it be, when they were as different as dawn from dusk and hardly looked like kin?

He and Walter resembled one another so little, in fact, that at the drunken send-off shindig Walter's friends had thrown—a bonfire gathering of folks who (if you didn't count Mike and Sully Latona) were all strangers to Jess—not one person had taken them for brothers. Likeable, easygoing Walter had the dark Cherokee eyes and the small, light frame of their mother's folks. Jess was six feet and seven inches, taller than any man in the valley, even their father. And as if the curse of absurd height had not already marked him as the peculiar son, nature had also given Jess a wiry bramble of hair, black as a crow's wing, and sunken eyes of the palest gray. "Hungry," a canny old woman selling lemonade at the county fair had once said of his eyes, "like a young Lincoln," after which he had started casting them mostly downward.

He made his way around the barn to the milking shed behind, mud sucking at his boots. Storms in the south had brought to the valley warm winds and an early thaw. He thought of climbing up to the loft and knocking back in the hay as Walter used to do, he was that weary. But it would never work and he knew it. When Walter had slept in the loft, Jess had always been tending to the herd. Left to wait, the cows would complain in voices loud enough to bring an irritated Clyde. Also, it was Thursday. Pat Badger would be pulling down the lane soon, wanting milk for the weekend. Not the sort of man you asked to stand by and watch you dig sleep out of your eyes.

Sage. That was how Jess's mother, Millie, described Pat. A single word, spoken as though she held an egg on her tongue, was somehow always closer to the point than Jess could get working with full sentences. Pat did take a keener, wider, more generous view of the world than most anyone else Jess knew. In fact, on another morning when Jess wasn't so cross, he might have sought counsel, asked the sage old farrier to see what he couldn't, which was how a fellow was supposed to live with any pleasure now that Walter wasn't going to come sliding into the milking shed of an evening, late as the dickens and cheerfully unrepentant. No working wisdom out of Pat today, though. Jess had no patience for it. The man had to be tapped like a great old tree, and the sap ran very slow.

The horses had heard him coming down the hill. Big Jake thumped on the stall door with his hoof and Maggie called out, shrill and insistent, demanding Jess stop by the tack room and dip his hand into the potbellied jar on the shelf. He ignored the pair. They knew full well Millie's ginger snaps were only given out in exchange for work. Some days they begged for them anyway. He ducked to miss the doorframe as he entered the milking shed and slipped quietly inside. The bawling of the cows only made him more eager for the peace the work of milking would bring. He set down the sanitizing buckets and began filling the troughs with fodder. When all was in readiness, he opened the lower door, letting in the noisy, complaining herd. The boss cow entered first. He greeted her as he always did, with a gentle slap on the rump. As she passed, he gazed over the bony crests of her hips to the valley stretched long and slender below the barn. Where the thin light caught the dew, the grass sparkled and glinted, as if the pasture had a sugar glaze.

So often at this hour, when the sun still hid behind the wall of Kerry Mountain, when the valley lay wrapped in the pale gray shadows of earliest dawn, Jess felt the thrill of a watcher, stealing in to witness a hidden, mystic rite. It pleased him to think that however old and practiced the ritual was now, it hadn't always been. A gawky young first night had once had to learn this graceful way of making an exit, of taking proper leave of the world, smoothly handing it off to the day.

It was just as this rite was ending that the light appeared. Before his eyes it shaped itself into a slender golden column, a beam such as he'd only seen once in his life, and that was in a picture on the wall of a neighbor's house. Long gone now, that family had been of some small religious sect looked at askance by valley folks, who were too taken up with eking a living from Prospect's rocky hills to worry over the exact day and hour of the second coming of Christ. It was to be a pretty rosy event, though, evidently, for the picture Jess had seen showed a blue-eyed, gentle-looking Jesus, riding barefoot out of heaven on a shining beam of light. Only that beam, as he remembered it, had pointed toward earth. This light shot up from the mountain peak—a single, radiant, upwardly moving stream that, once it reached the sky (a sky now in bright, blinding glow), seemed to rend the fabric of it and continue on, as if seeking a destination beyond the visible world.

"Glory," Jess said, a word that echoed around the quiet valley as unexpected as the light.

Glory. Not a word he used, customarily. It was the right one, though, for now that he had spoken it, the light appeared to shimmer, gleaming a darker, richer gold against the yellow brightness of the sky.

It began to dance.

And while it danced—the entire amber-lit length of it quivering in a holy, grace-filled shimmy—Jess watched, keeping as still as he could manage. His legs were trembling, his heart beat hard against his ribs, causing his breaths to grow short and quick, and his palms had begun to sweat. But he had a strong urge to stay put, to keep silent and wait. For what, he would never be able with any certainty to say. A pronouncement of some kind, perhaps. The song of an otherworldly choir. Whatever it was never materialized.

The feeling of expecting it would be with him a long, long time.

"Shekinah Light."

At the sound of his father's voice, Jess turned and saw Clyde coming out of the shed, watched as he ducked his head for the overhang, crossed in two strides the path between them, and came to stand next to Jess. Shoulder to shoulder, they gazed at the scene. The dance was over. The light was fading now, but still visible as it hovered above the mountain.

"I've never seen it, mind," Clyde said, in the same flat voice he used to mention a possibility of rain, "only heard. God himself, the old folks used to say it was, paying some lucky devil a visit. It's a sun pillar. Just ice crystals way up in the atmosphere, reflecting the light of the rising sun."

From the corner of his eye, Jess checked his father's face, measuring his expression against the cut of his statement. He wished to find a hint of wonder in those level gray eyes, just the barest flicker of awe, but the man was gone. Clyde was inside the milking shed already, affectionately cussing the cows as he locked them in the stanchions. Soon the shed got quiet. His father had begun the washing. A scrupulous bathing of all the udders while the water in the sanitizing buckets was still hot and the cows were going contentedly at their fodder.

The yolk-colored sun was well above the peak now and the beam was fading, almost gone. This was all right with Jess, for the spell was broken anyhow. He turned and went into the shed, bending his long legs and ducking his head as he entered, just as his father had done. The two had not received their height from Edward Hazel, Clyde's great-grandfather, who had built the house and barn. Nor had it come from Raleigh, Edward's son, who later built the long, low-slung milking shed—an odd decision for the time, and one that had surely caused people to wonder if he had lost all good Hazel sense. There were farms now in their part of Pennsylvania, the western part, that were specialized, but not then. In those days farms existed mostly to sustain themselves, and only when that end was certain did they profit on the excess.

It was Raleigh's shed that had fated all Hazels to be dairymen. Jess knew it was because Clyde never let his sons forget: "Do you see how important your actions are?"

Jess had to smile, thinking of this, for he could almost hear his brother's voice. Walter was asking him to recall the time Clyde had got on the subject during morning chores.

Jess and Walter had just got the milking underway when Walter mentioned he was going to need the outhouse soon. He had no more finished saying it when their father walked in. Seeing the look on Clyde's face, Jess had taken a firmer grip on the teats of his cow and sat straighter on his stool, for his father hated to see him slouch. And as always, he had worried for his brother, who never worried a straw for himself. He'd been so glad that Walter had not left his chores and gone up the hill, as he had said he might. Clyde stood like a tree in the door. Some worry, either past or future, had been gnawing at him that morning, for he began in the usual way—abruptly, as if Walter and Jess had been in on his thoughts, helping him stir the stew.

"You boys just have no idea how your every move affects the family."

At that, Walter had snickered—softly, so only Jess could hear.

"It's time you two started using more care, got some direction before going and doing a thing. Especially you, Walter, as the oldest." Clyde stepped inside, positioning himself so he could see both Jess and Walter, each seated at the side of his own cow.

Jess could not see Walter's expression, but had no doubt it was as innocent as a baby's.

"In fact, Walter," Clyde said, "before you go to make another move, I want you to see me first. Let me consider it awhile."

Walter always had his wits about him. Even as a boy of thirteen. He had held back from replying, letting the tension build, the only sounds in the shed being those made by the cows—tails whipping up to swat flies, the quiet slap and swish of thick wet tongues washing down the feed trough—and just when Jess didn't think he could take it another second, Walter had said, in a voice as straight as string,

"Say I did want to make a move, Father. Wanted it bad. How much time would you need to consider? I mean, just how long is a while?"

Jess was used to such jokes, being generally the butt of them. If he could have seen the insolent glint in his brother's eyes, the telltale sign that Walter's lithe brain was working at a jest, he might have been ready. But he couldn't see the glint, couldn't see Walter at all, and when the question came, delivered with perfect, comic soberness, Jess had to fake a coughing fit to cover his laughter. He was sober, now, remembering his father's red face. You just never knew if Clyde would grin and ask to be let in on the joke, allowing Walter's humor to settle light on them all, or turn and stride away, causing chores to proceed in silence so thick you could cut it with a knife. That morning it had been the latter.

He fetched a milking stool and set it absently under a cow. Lord, how he missed that way Walter had of dealing with Clyde. Though he could not change his mood—not even Millie could do that—Walter could always find a way to alkalize it, a thing Jess had no talent for. He leaned in, resting his head against the cow's warm side, closing his eyes. He saw again the beautiful, shimmying light and heard his father's voice, mocking an innocent faith. He felt cheated. As a youngster he had often wished to have a swarthy complexion and a governor put on his shooting frame, so he might be mistaken for one of his friend Mike's many siblings. The Latona family was large and loud and unabashedly religious. They were good Sicilian Catholics who baptized their fat, dark babies and confirmed their daughters and took their sons to the priest for a blessing before sending them off to war. Clyde was a pacifist, of course, a remnant of his Quaker past. He didn't hold to war. But Walter had gone to be a soldier regardless. And Jess couldn't help thinking things might be different if he'd done it with a blessing. Anyway, how could anyone be sure God wasn't here, milling about the valley?

No doubt his father was right. Clyde always was. The beam of light probably was an extraordinary reflection of the everyday sun, but did that mean it couldn't also be more? It might also be a kind of ladder, the means for God to get down to this patch of soil Hazels had been working since old Penn first claimed these woods and set things back to the way they used to be.

Jess realized, of course, that the farm didn't compare to stopping over at the Latona house, where a divine visitor might at least be recognized, everyone talking at once and Rita yelling from the kitchen that He should wipe His feet on the mat. But the Hazels were decent folks. They worked hard. Surely that counted for something. Things wouldn't need to be exactly normal either (Jess had no wish to be greedy), just as much like the old life as could be managed, under the circumstances. Walter was gone. And in the last several weeks, Mother's letters to him had brought no reply, only a new uncertainty. It lay over the valley now, thick as a winter fog. The Hazel family, fortress of steadiness and reliability, had proved as vulnerable as any other. That couldn't be put right. Jess yawned and reached for the near teats of his cow. But some sort of cosmic resetting of the farm's clock to a regular cycle of work and rest might be a start toward pretending it could be.

2

Kerry Mountain
Prospect, Pennsylvania
May 1, 1952
5:56 AM

Eli Zook ran his hands through his hair, rose from the chair he had been occupying off and on since dusk the day before, and walked stiffly across the room to the window. Sunlight had begun to filter through the curtain, and he wanted to slide it back along the rod and let it in. The night was done at last, if the trouble it had ushered in was not. It seemed an especially bright, bold ray that sliced through the dingy pane, instantly bathing the room in light. But then, mornings came sudden to this peak, he had learned. No gradual lightening of the eastern sky. No soft, downy light hatching out from the wing of the horizon. There was only this sun, full-grown and robust. He sighed, an ache for home swelling his chest. How he yearned to be there again, if only once, to see the quiet approach of dawn, to watch the slow retreat of the shadows from the fields. An Amish sun knew how to arrive in good Plain order.

He lowered the lamp's wick, snuffing the flame, and gazed down at the girl in the bed. She lay still with eyes closed, drawing quiet breaths. It was the muscles flexing at the hinge of her jaw that told him she was tensed. She was ready.

Her last cry still rang in his ears, but Eli was listening now for another sound. It was not unfamiliar, the noise downstairs. Knuckles against wood. An insistent muffled pounding. But it had been a long while since he'd heard it. Maria cried out again and struggled to sit up. Her dark eyes were open now and fastened on his face. Eli turned and came back to stand by the bed. He bent to her, arranging the pillows and rolled-up quilts so they supported her back. All of this he did with a measure of caution. At the peak of a pain she was like a wounded dog and flinched at his touch. In its wake, though, she would turn to him as she might to a husband or lover, glazed eyes seeking his. Then she would stretch out her hand and clutch at his sleeve, muttering to him, tears gathered like drops of dew on the tips of her eyelashes. Whether her words cursed or blessed, Eli did not know. She suffered in her language, not his. When she was quiet again, he wiped her brow with the cloth he had been using to moisten her parched tongue and cool her cheeks, listening the while to the knocking downstairs as it grew louder, more insistent. And when it did not cease, he pressed the cloth into her hand and backed by inches from the room, severing her gaze with the bedroom door.

The kitchen was dark still, the one window in it opened west, and he had left the lamp upstairs. He opened the door and peered out. The wide shadow on the other side of the screen spoke, a deep male voice.

"Everything all right in there?"

"Yah."

"You sure, mister? I'm not saying you'd lie, but I'm pretty familiar with the sound of a female in distress."

"Yah? You a doctor?"

"Not a doctor. A farrier. On my way down to the Hazel place for milk. My Peggy wants it fresh and Jesse, that's Clyde's youngest, will milk right into the pail for me. Doesn't come any fresher than that, I tell her, 'less you're a suckling calf. Anyhow, I got a queer urge to come up this way, saw you had a horse tethered out by your shed. Either there's a panicked mare upstairs, or your woman is getting close. You got help, or no?"

"Nah."

"You want any?"

Eli hesitated, just as the girl cried out again. The man was not waiting for an answer now. He jerked the screen door open and plowed through it, brushing Eli aside with ease. Once he was inside the kitchen, he stopped and stood still with head cocked, as if listening for the long scream that floated down directly from above. Even as it pierced the air, he was turning on his heel in that direction. The floorboards groaned as he lumbered into the hallway, tossing his hat and coat aside as he went, and vanished.

Eli went to the table and sank into a chair. For three days, he had struggled and worked to rein in his thoughts, threatening every minute to bolt. How he had managed to keep vigil with Maria all last night, he did not know. He only knew he was drained of all such power now, so frail feeling and limp in his limbs, as if the days and nights had been spent in a hot high fever that at last was broken.

The farrier had found the room. The big raw voice turned gentle as a midwife's as he first consoled her, then questioned. Her answers, when she found the breath, told Eli that she had decided already to put her trust in the man. He wondered if her mutterings had been prayers and she believed the man to be heaven sent.

Eli listened as the farrier's voice became a low, encouraging rumble. They were a team now in earnest. Listening, his head grew heavy. Maria had, after all, no more need of him. The little help he could give her, clumsy words and clumsier ministrations, was useless now that the big farrier had come. And there was no use in fretting, worrying whether the man was the sort who would talk. It was too late for that. And somehow Eli had a strange certainty he wasn't. Each of these thoughts eased his mind a little, and yet a little more, until he stopped fighting his weariness altogether. Making a cradle of his arms, he lowered his head into it, the sound of her laboring soothing him, like the fury of a storm way off in the distance.

He woke to the weight of a hand lying firm on his shoulder. He looked up to see that sunlight slanted through the kitchen window. A man stood over him, as big and broad as an upright ox, judgment glinting in his clear blue eyes.

"Don't exactly seem like you've been wearing the floor out down here." The man took his hand from Eli's shoulder and crossed one arm over the other, muscles straining against the fabric of his gray cotton shirt. Blood stained his turned-up sleeves. His expression was hard. "I've got four boys. And each time I slept nary a wink. Not until a babe was stowed safe in his mother's arms."

Eli rubbed a hand over his eyes, his brain fogged with weariness. The man seemed real enough. But why was he here? Why did he stand in Eli's kitchen talking of boys, and of his wife giving birth? Then he remembered that Maria was in labor. And that her labor had collided with one of his spells. It was over now, the spell—it had run a short course all on its own (Maria too focused on her own pain to quiet him with a song). The fair that had set up twirling and hawking inside his head had closed down, departed at last. But he didn't hope for rest. There was none of that to be had. For his sort of weary, sleep must always suffice. Even as the man stood over him and the stained sleeves and the terrible quiet upstairs pricked needle-sharp at the edges of his mind, his lethargy returned, sudden and powerful. His head was a burden, his neck too flimsy to support the weight of it. He had only one thought, one desire, and that was to lay it back down in the comforting circle of his arms. If only the man wasn't still there, still talking.

"It was a fight," the farrier was saying. "One the bitty thing meant to win. She came feet first, eyes open, looking straight into mine. Little hoot-owl eyes. Wiselike. If you know what I mean." He peered at Eli, his blue eyes narrowed, then shrugged. "Gave me a queer, queer feeling, that's all I know," he said. "That same feeling got me up here this morning. Could be punchy, I guess, but it doesn't seem now like stopping at your place was my idea at all. I'm going." He rolled down his sleeves, unmindful of the stains, and put on his coat. He glanced around the kitchen, looking for his cap, still lying on the floor by the stairs where he had tossed it. He picked it up and set it on his head, settling it low on his brow. "You want me to go by Doc Bloom's and have him come look in on them?"

Eli roused. "No doctor," he said.

The man looked hard at him again, blue eyes sharp. Then he shrugged, spreading his hands.

"Your business, mister. I'm aware you'uns got your own ways of doing." His gaze went then to Eli's suspenders, flicked over the homespun shirt and buttoned fly, and Eli knew that this farrier was a man who did not judge, unless it was correctly. "That pride won't serve you near so well out here among us English, though. I'll warn you that. The girl is weak. Weaker than she ought to be. She hadn't the strength to bring a child into this world on her own. If the little 'un hadn't a been so all-fired ready and I hadn't happened by the way I did, I believe you'd be passing a grim morning. But she sings the same tune as you. No doctor." He opened the door and stepped onto the porch. "I don't hold to pressing folks against their will," he said, through the screen. "So, I'm not pressing, just advising. You ought to get Doc Bloom."

"The first thing you said was the right one," Eli said, getting up from the table. He locked the screen door, snapping the brass hook into its eye. "It is my business."

"Don't worry, mister. I've said my piece," the farrier said. "A more generous piece, folks will tell you, than I'm used to parceling out." He turned to go. At the step he halted and turned back. "That's a pretty trotter you've got tied up out there," he said. "Ten-year-old, I'm guessing, though she could as easily be twelve. How long since she foundered?"

"Last week."

"Well you did right, tethering. Keep her off that rich grass. At least until I can get back up here. No feed either. Sweet or otherwise. Hay and plenty of clean fresh water, that's all. You won't mind, I guess, me stopping off in the next day or two and seeing to her feet?"

"Yah. I don't mind."

"Good. So long, then."

Once again, the man stopped at the step, turned around, and came back to the door.

"Come pretty near to forgetting my manners. Congratulations, Mr. . . ."

"Zook. Eli Zook."

"Pat Badger." The man grinned, his expression turning friendly. "I'd ask you to unlock that screen and shake hands, but I fear it would seem like backing up, seeing as we've been pretty well acquainted already by circumstance. Don't know what it signifies, Mr. Zook, a child choosing this day to get born. But it does seem fitting, someway, for that fey-eyed one upstairs. As I said before, congratulations. She's a fine posy for your basket."

3

JESS WAS ALONE IN THE BARN, working over Maggie's tack, when Pat Badger finally eased in, looking tired but pleased. The farrier's wide chest was caved in a way Jess knew well—that good, spent-shouldered slump of a man who has just finished some hard but satisfying work. He had seen Clyde look that way, generally when a calf he'd given up for dead slipped alive into the world and began to try out its legs.

"We've stripped all the cows, Pat," Jess said. "And Father's gone out to the Amish already with the milk."

"And what am I to do then?"

Jess grinned.

"I reckon you could go by the supermarket on your way home and get some store-bought. Pour it into Peggy's pail and see if she's the wiser."

"Oh, she'd be the wiser," Pat said, dryly. "And if she wasn't, her cats would be. She's got six now, you know, all Siamese. Petty, tattling creatures."

He turned and went into the cooler, where he knew he would find Peggy's milk. When he had filled his pail, he came back and leaned against the tack room door, watching Jess. Pat never lingered. Jess decided the farrier must have something on his mind and stayed quiet, kneading soap into the collar seams with his thumb, a little self-consciously now. He often watched Pat at this work, but he could not recall that it had ever been the other way around. The rag, which had been slipping smoothly over the collar before, began under Pat's keen gaze to drag and catch until at last Jess lost his rhythm altogether. He set the collar aside.

"What's the day brought you so far, Pat?"

"Miracles, mostly," Pat said, with a slow, broad grin. "And some burden," he added, turning sober. "One doesn't come without the other, you know."

"I don't know," Jess said. "Burdens, I've got some experience with. Miracles, not so much. Although, now that you mention it, I thought I had one on the line this morning. Turned out to be a trick of the sun."

"It was a wonder of a dawn, wasn't it?" Pat said. The grin returned, wider than before. "'He is beautiful and radiant with great splendor. Of You, Most High, he bears the likeness.'"

"I've heard that," Jess said. "Or I should say, I've read it. On a plaque at Latona's Deli. It's a prayer, isn't it? By some saint or other. But you're not Catholic."

"It's a hymn. And no, I'm not Catholic. But neither was the man who first sang it out. Not the way I see it. Attach the word to a fellow like Francis of Assisi, and it becomes a tag in his ear. Before, he was free as God. Now, because of the tag, he's owned by men who sift his every word and deed through their soft white hands. Wheat, they say. Or chaff. But for them, it's the sifting that's important."

While he talked, Jess listened, curious. There was an odd spark in Pat's eye today. And he had never known the man to bring forth so many words at once without pause.

"Peggy's Presbyterian, isn't she?"

"Methodist, but that's splitting hairs. Hand me those reins, Jesse. I hate to be idle."

When he had passed the reins and a soaped rag over to Pat, Jess picked up the collar and went back to kneading the leather into the suppleness that lent it strength. They sat for a while then in comfortable silence, Jess stealing occasional envious glances at Pat's huge hands, working soap over the reins with absentminded ease, like a hoary old fiddler rosining his bow.

"Do Methodists have saints?" he said, after a few minutes.

Pat chuckled. "Lord, no. Peg'd have your scalp for suggesting it. They've just got good Bible-believing folks in her church." He shook his head. "But there's plenty of sifting goes on."

"Are you one of those?"

"What? A Bible believer?"

"Yes."

"Well, now," Pat said, with a sideways glance at Jess, his hands still going at the reins, "I generally view that as a trick question. Most folks who ask it have got reasons other than curiosity, which tends to incline me not to answer. But you aren't asking what they are. I know that. And I don't mind admitting to you," he glanced around the barn, as if his wife might somehow be listening, "that there are Scriptures I hold very dear. Especially the Psalms. All on earth that strikes me as good or wearies my soul nigh to death once also moved an ancient scribe, and he set it down in words. That, to me, is a marvelous thing. And I don't take it lightly." Pat paused, looking up from his work. "What about you, Jesse? Are you a Bible man?"

"I guess not. Mother's kin were foot-washers back in Kentucky. She keeps the old Jenkins Bible on a shelf in the front room. Walter and I used to take it down and look at it sometimes when we were kids. He knew where to find the parts Mother would never have let us read if it was any other book. Kings, one and two. Song of Solomon. The two of us had some pretty good times with those. But I've never much read it on my own."

Jess happened to look toward the barn door just then and gave a guilty start. There was his father, coming through it. He had made awfully good time, getting to the cheese factory at New Wilmington and back already. Jess's cheeks burned. He didn't like to think his father might have heard him asking what Clyde would consider silly, womanish questions of the family farrier. Pat's expression had turned sober. He handed the halter to Jess and stood up. "I need a word, Clyde. If you've got time," he said.

Pat had not stayed just to be companionable, Jess realized, and left the men to their business. He gathered up the harness pieces and took them into the tack room. When he had finished stowing the tack away and came out, the two had left the barn. He looked out and saw them walking away together toward Pat's truck. They made a curious pair of figures. Alike, and yet not. Set across their heads a flat stick would surely measure horizontal, but through the shoulders Pat made two of Clyde.

Jess turned the horses out to graze and went to work mucking stalls. It was a daily chore with all the rain. A pair of draft horses confined to stall made a mess directly proportionate to their size. As he passed the open barn door, he caught sight of Maggie.

"What's your rush?" he called out to her, laughing.

Out to pasture for the first time in days, she stepped as unhurriedly as ever, picking her way down the hill toward the tenderest new grass.

Clyde was a Percheron man, partial to the breed for their willing, cautious nature and careful feet. Pat raised Clydesdales. His horses were not known for their ability to work, which was likely to be considerable, but for their beauty and form. Pat shipped them far and wide to rich folks who coveted them for show. As far as Jess knew, his father was the only non-Amish farmer left in Butler County who still used horsepower in his fields. Machines guzzled gas and belched exhaust and broke down in the field when the sun was still high overhead. That was not progress, Clyde insisted, but a foolish waste of hard-earned cash. Once established, grass grew free for the cutting. And a draft horse came designed for hard work.

After the war, a county extension agent, fresh from the university and full of zeal, had come out to Hazel Valley, Jess remembered, to get Clyde in step with the times. The future of dairy farming lay in mechanized milking, the agent said. It was the only answer for a population so rapidly on the rise. Why, the entire industry was about bust wide open. Clyde had better think about getting on board. Jess's father had looked at the agent as if he spoke in a foreign tongue.

"Industry? What industry? I'm in the business of keeping my own family fed. And my neighbor's, if there's a need. He does the same, and his neighbor does likewise. I'll be straight with you, son. It's a mighty satisfactory arrangement. So, unless you've got something more than higher yields and lowered contentment to offer, we can take our leave of one another now. That sound you hear is my cows, begging me to lay my unprogressive hands on them and ease them of their milk."

The agent had gone away thwarted, a look of utter confusion on his face as he got into his truck and departed from Hazel Valley. When they were alone again, Clyde had turned to Jess, laying a hand on his neck, and said, "We've not seen the last of that fellow, Jesse boy, and if I know anything, there will be more just like him. Pay heed now, because this place will be yours someday."

And Jess had smiled and said, "Mine and Walter's."

He was twelve then, young enough that he still believed, still dreamed. Of his own house nestled into the rise of the hill above the northwest forty. Of working the fields with his horses while Walter tended their dairy herd. Of their wives, sitting together on the porch at twilight, snapping beans and gossiping. And of their children, hunting the nests of field mice and rabbits among the rows of drying hay, pleading, as their fathers used to do, for the nests to be spared when the time for baling came.

"We'll see about Walter," Clyde had said, hardness creeping into his voice. "Your brother doesn't have our zeal for this life, you know. There's red blood in his veins. We've got dirt in ours, you and me."

Jess's skinny chest had swelled with pride, then contracted again at the thought that Father might have it right about Walter.

"Machines make factories, Jesse," his father had said then, getting back to his subject, "not farms. A good farm knows its size. And the best farm has eyes no bigger than its stomach. If you can remember that, you'll do well."

Of course, all that the agent had prophesied had speedily come to pass. These days, everyone got their milk from the big mechanized dairies, and Clyde was left selling his to the Amish for cheese.

The stalls were emptied now, scraped down to the clay floor. Jess laid down a thickness of clean straw and wheeled the muck cart out to the manure pile. West of the barn, Pat's old blue Ford truck went ambling down the lane. Clyde was walking up the hill to the house, a grim look on his face. He wondered what Pat had needed to see his father about. And if it had anything to do with what had kept him from coming around at milking time. Perhaps it had something to do with what burdens he'd said the morning had brought. He thought then of Pat's miracles and grinned. He had snuck up to the house that morning and looked in the encyclopedia. The light was just what Clyde had said it was, tiny particles of ice, reflecting the rays of the rising sun.

And it *had* danced.

4

SPRING WAS LONGER THAT YEAR THAN MOST, or so it seemed to Jess. Wetter too. Perhaps in part because of his mother's sadness. The summer that followed was more the usual kind, each day a single blazing fire set to burn through the working hours and die out at dusk. Of a morning, Jess wore his coat in the barn. The nights were that cool.

In late July, more than a year since he'd gone away, they finally got word of Walter. Missing. Presumed dead.

There was no strife on the first floor after the telegram came to keep Jess awake at night. But it was a dread silence that took its place, and he almost wished for its return. His mother had ceased to speak his brother's name, or very nearly—a change that troubled Jess no end. When he did chance to hear Millie talking of her eldest, it was plain that Walter had become the child of her remembering heart, not the son of her future.

Then, in the wake of a slow, dry autumn without beauty or marked change, it was suddenly winter, and Jess had no more need to fret over what was, or was not, being said downstairs between his folks. He dropped all pretense of hope for Walter's return from Korea too. It was of no use. His mother was gone.

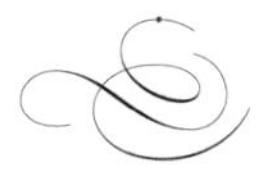

"It was only natural and right, the way it happened," Jess said to Margit Busco, the neighbor who tried hard to keep him fed during the first shocked, muted days of his orphaning.

Margit was one-half of a pair of widowed sisters-in-law the Hazels had always only ever referred to as the Hungarians. Clyde and Millie had not been friendly with the two women, who kept goats on the back porch and chickens under the front and hawked their garden harvest from a stand on the highway, but Jess had always liked them, if mostly in secret. And he had never been gladder to see anyone than on those nights he came up from the barn to find Margit in his kitchen reheating beef stroganoff, or cabbage rolls or cauliflower soup or whatever else she had fed her two small grandsons for dinner. He was glad not just for the food, but for Margit's stocky stolid presence, which hushed, if only for an hour or two, the echo of the empty house. If Margit had no hopeful word to say, she was likely to say nothing at all. It was perhaps this trait that Jess liked most in the old woman, for hers was a companionable silence, altogether different from that of his ghosts.

When she was sure Jess had eaten all he wanted, though it was never as much as she thought he should, Margit would take a glass down from the cabinet, rinse the coffee from Jess's cup, and pour them each a drink. And with his tongue loosened by whiskey, Jess would find himself talking about his folks.

"They were a team," he'd say, leaning in close, so as not to shout while speaking of the dead.

His dead.

Margit was hard of hearing in one ear and only grasped a little English with the other, and Jess would have developed a strong need by then, his cup being almost empty, to make sure she not only heard but also understood. He wished her to know just how fitting it was for Clyde and Millie to be in the truck together when it slipped the road at Old Line Bridge.

Nobody saw it happen, but Jess had with his tireless imagination viewed the scene of the accident in his mind a thousand times since: watched in slow motion his mother's small, slender fingers uncurl from her lap as she reached for the door handle, saw his father's black eyebrows form a thick, wondering knot as he felt the loss of control in the steering wheel, understood too late that the truck's tires were leaving the road. Had there been any last declarations of devotion or asking forgiveness of one another as they waited for the frigid waters of the Beaver River in January to close tight their steel tomb? Jess had his doubts. He knew for sure there were no prayers echoing around the truck cab, no desperate pleas for divine assistance. If the folks could have hired the Creator to lend them a hand, paid him a good, fair wage to pluck them from the icy flow, well, that would have been all right, and they might have agreed to it. Anything else was charity. And that was not the Hazel way.

"A team, I tell you," Jess would say again, anxiously seeking Margit's faded blue eyes with his own. "As solid a working pair as Maggie and Big Jake."

And Margit would listen, quietly drinking. Then, without a word, she would drain the whiskey from her glass, and going to the sink she would rinse it, drying it carefully with a towel before putting it back in the cupboard. All this while Jess waited, agonized, for her to nod and agree. In the end, she would, though she could not seem to manage it looking him in the eye.

"Sure, they was, Jesse," she would finally say, reaching politely for his cup. "Sure they was."

5

FOR FIVE YEARS JESS LIVED as if he had been marooned alone in his own valley. A castaway. The farm his lonesome island. He ran the dairy wholly on his own steam, and worked his fields in solitude, except for those few days in summer when he would hire help for the haying. A man if he could get one. Two boys if he couldn't. In later years, when his long, straight legs had begun to bow a little and his joints often ached, he would look back and marvel at the callous way he had treated his young body.

"Not a drop of mercy," he would exclaim then. "Too young, I guess, to realize there would only be the one."

And he would shake his head. Gently. Sympathetically. As if he were recalling someone else's life.

At the time, though, he had no such compassion. He worked his limbs as if they were forged of iron, stopping only when to not do so became absurd. He never would have used a horse as hard.

He moved through the days as if through mud. Morning and evening, the cows still made their way up the hill to the barn, complaining to Jess of bags stretched to discomfort. Only now he greeted the herd (his herd) in silence. He milked as dutifully as ever but took little of the old pleasure in hearing the tinny first thwack of milk against the bucket, the knowledge that he gave a cow ease. When the snow had gone, and the sun leaned nearer the earth and all was freshened and new, he stood along his tilled and planted fields and saw the sight every farmer covets: small green fingers unfolding to the light. Evidence of viable seed. Proof he hasn't sown in vain. The sight hardly moved him. Nowhere near, anyway, to his old glee.

Then one morning the fog lifted from the upper pasture and he found one of his heifers tending the still, limp body of her first calf. When he squatted beside the calf, he saw a reason to hope: a web of amniotic material covered its mouth and nose. A swift swipe of his palm over its face and the membrane had been whisked away, but the calf did not breathe, so he reached up and snapped a twig from the sycamore the cow had calved under, and bent to the calf with it, tickling its pale blue nostrils. Anytime a stillborn calf suddenly shook itself and lived was a sure thrill for Jess, always filled him with a marvelous, springing-up awareness of kinship with all that lived and breathed on earth. This calf—it was a little heifer—did all that. She sneezed and coughed and even, with encouragement from the cow, struggled to her feet. But though Jess stood by waiting for it, the old feeling never came.

Its absence unnerved him.

Whether an animal lived or died, it was all the same evidence of nature's resilience. Both Clyde and Pat had always insisted that, in rare agreement. But to Jess, watching the calf suckle with an encouraging vigor only an hour after her birth, it seemed only to reveal a fickle nature. This life was a struggle. That, he knew well. It was a mighty one too, some days. But any hardship that had come had always seemed balanced by a certain joy: that of courting the earth and having her yield. It was real wealth, joy. The heart of the whole thing, to his mind. He'd always felt richer than his friends who lived in town, who knew no more of husbandry than to weed the backyard garden or water a strip of lawn, had secretly pleasured in knowing that his was a life of privilege.

The calf was sated, her belly full of colostrum. She collapsed in the grass to sleep. Next to her, the cow began placidly to graze. Jess turned away, satisfied that the heifer was going to mother naturally, no further help from him. He was glad, but gladness did not lift the uneasiness that had descended. He felt strange. Suddenly off kilter.

As if he'd struck out across ground that looked level but wasn't. Even when the folks were alive, and Walter was not fighting a war or presumed dead, and they had all been as knit as a glove, Jess had been given to bouts of light melancholy, the consequence of living too much in his own head, of too many conversations had only with himself. But he had no experience with discontent. To be so suddenly ill at ease with this life he loved was to be abruptly vacated. Emptied of even the plainest pleasure. If on this morning in his pasture nature had chanced to be kind, Jess felt no urge to gloat.

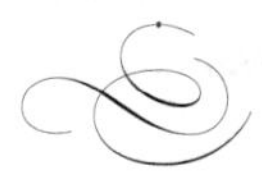

Sleep was elusive. Now more than ever. It came only with exhaustion.

Jess was troubled by dreams—vague waking fears that rearranged themselves into worrisome, realistic scenes as he slept. To avoid them, he took to staying up very late, his eyes bulging from weariness and nerves.

The electric light his mother had so coveted, pleased as a child on Christmas morn when the first pole appeared in the valley, was distasteful to him now. It glared. Exposed. Revealed his lone state. For the darkest hours he would light an oil lamp, staying in the small, kind circle of its glow until milking time, reading as if his life depended on it *The Journals of Lewis and Clark.*

The Journals were a onetime Christmas present to Walter from an aunt who lived way off in California. She did not know her sister's boys. Not well enough, anyhow, to know that of the two of them only Jess read for pleasure. And since Walter was never one to hoard what he had no use for, he'd turned around and given the books to Jess, handing them off with an appalling lack of ceremony. No more than the previous year when Jess had been tossed a paperback copy of *Tarzan of the Apes*. Jess often wished on a fevered sleepless night that he could thank Walter for his gift, however offhand it had been. For when Clark wrote in spare, terse language of the descent of a mosquito horde, or Lewis described, using far more words than Clark would have needed, how the days of relentless rain had affected morale, it gave Jess's mind rest. The only form it would accept to take.

It was on one of those nights as he read, making his way across the plains to Mandan country, that he came across a paragraph that stirred his mind up instead of bedding it down. By the time he finished reading it, the passage had kindled a fire he did not know whether to try and snuff out or tend and feed:

> *Along the northern sky was a large space occupied by a light of a pale but brilliant white colour: which rising from the horizon, extended itself to nearly twenty degrees above it. After glittering for some time its colours would be overcast, and almost obscured, but again it would burst out with renewed beauty; the uniform colour was pale light, but its shapes were various and fantastic: at times the sky was lined with light coloured streaks rising perpendicularly from the horizon, and gradually expanding into a body of light which we could trace the floating columns sometimes advancing sometimes retreating and shaping into infinite forms, the space in which they moved. It all faded away before the morning.*

At the end of the passage, Jess sat stunned, staring blankly at the page. He read it again. And again.

He read the passage again, three times through, before closing the book and setting it aside. He sat still and quiet for a while, gathering himself. And when he felt strong enough, he rose from his chair, walked across the room, sinking to his knees as he reached the window, and leaned heavily against the sill. Only a few steps, but when he looked back across the space, it seemed a great accomplishment. A pilgrimage, of sorts, finished on his knees. Outside the moon shone full and bright, beckoning his gaze. He raised his hands to part the curtains and saw that his fingers were trembling. As he looked out, gazing across the valley to Kerry Mountain, he could see as if it were yesterday and not five years ago the pillar of light. "Glory," he recalled saying. And now, in a hoarse whisper, he spoke the word again.

"Glory."

He was certain now of its rightness. Captains Clark and Lewis had no doubt spoken it too, caught in the presence of the lights.

He was too keyed up now to read. Peering through the curtain sheer, he saw that the moon still beckoned. He went out and stood for a moment on the porch, running his hands through his hair, grasping for the meaning in it all. Wondering if it had any. Worried that it might not. Scared as hell that it surely did. After a little while, he made his way down the hill to the barn and climbed the stairs to the hayloft, throwing open the hay doors to the night. Still weak in the knees, he sank to the hard plank floor, sitting on his heels to gaze out, gripping his thighs with white-knuckled hands. And as he watched the thin, silent clouds rush across the purple sky, Clyde's voice rose to his ear.

"God himself, the old folks thought it was."

There had been no proof that morning of any such visitation. Not once the light pillar had vanished. But Jess had been privy to something miraculous. Of that, he had no doubt. Yet it harrowed too, the light, had been haunting him ever since, as if that had been its whole purpose for flashing down. Now he couldn't help wondering just how much glory, and not the grief that followed, had sapped his joy. He was acutely aware, suddenly, of a rattling emptiness beneath his ribs.

A hollowness. And he knew the kernel that had once filled the space must have been withering a long time.

Not from the day they'd got word of Walter. Not from the day of the accident.

From the moment the light appeared above the valley.

It was a mournful, mournful thought. Even as he had it, the moon appeared to dim, glowing softer, kinder, as if to say gently, compassionately, that Jess had finally got it right.

The whole thing saddened him so much he wanted to cry.

Sadder still was knowing he couldn't.

There had been times in the last five years when Jess had craved tears more powerfully than a poor man longs for wealth. Why they insisted on staying locked away, forever paining his tight, squeezed throat, he could not fathom. It seemed absurd to be dry-eyed with so much reason to weep. Peggy Badger, good woman, had assured him at the funeral, her thumb fruitlessly circling his cheek in search of a tear, that it was a known trait of Hazel men. They literally could not weep. At about eighteen, she insisted, or however old Jess was now, they lost the ability—the ducts grew over or something. Her words moved his heart. Jess was grateful, and yet hardly reassured. (Though, admittedly, he had never seen his father cry.) For Clyde was dead, having been the only full-grown Hazel man Jess had ever known. As it stood now, Jess could only take his own lack of tears to be proof that his theory was correct. He was evaporating. Would soon be as dry as an old husk. If, as he suspected, a secret, *the* secret, perhaps, deep and primeval, was being passed across the air tonight, if God had His lips to the ear of the moon, Jess intended to overhear it.

Deep into the night, he waited, kneeling on the hard floor of the loft, staring down the moon. But aside from the distant bark of a fox, he heard nothing. And yet he lingered, staying until the cows began to low, signaling dawn. The day's work began to shape up in his mind then, edging mystery out. But when the moon waxed full again, he returned. Inexplicably drawn. Vaguely hopeful. Until at last, one cold starless night, when the moon hung huge and low and soft in the sky, he gave up his quest.

It was the moon's nearness that did it. Remaining so aloof in such proximity, she seemed to gently mock. And with sudden, stunning clarity, he saw himself for exactly what he was—a fool. The only state worse than death, his father had believed. Jess didn't need answers. There was no mystery. The moon still gazed down, but now her eyes were craters. Dark sterile pits, carved into the moon's surface, probably by asteroids. He laughed mirthlessly, shaking his head at his own foolishness. And as he laughed, the sound echoing eerie and ghostlike around the loft, Jess found himself pulled in the direction of the loft door as if by a wire, long legs sliding across the barn floor, feet shuffling his body forward until the toes of his boots hung over the edge, until there was nothing between him and the sky, hard ground twenty feet below. The wires pulled once more and his arms stretched wide, stretched until his fingers touched the door frame on each side. And suddenly, Jess was leaning out. A great blue heron, ready for flight. Years passed. A thousand moons rose and set. Or so it seemed to him, as he hung over the darkness. Waiting. Wondering. Until at last he knew. In three swift motions he stepped back from the opening, closed the hay doors, and locked them tight, burying the loft in pitch blackness. In the whole of his life, Jess Hazel had never been, nor would he ever be again, so sure—so assured—as he was in that moment. With the slow, careful deliberation of the blind, he turned and felt his way back down the stairs.

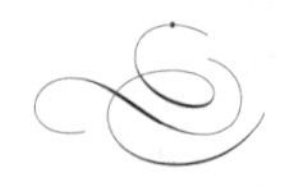

Now that he knew how it was a man should live, it was clear that it was no more than his lot to do so. He still grieved, still felt acutely the pain of his aloneness. But there was a great deal of solace, he found, in taking Clyde's approach to existence. Acceptance had its own plain reward. To be sure, living in such a way, a man's sense of wonder was muted. But so was his sense of tragedy. Jess did not pine now for the old joy or wish for knowledge beyond his ken. And except for that which he now put in himself, and that which ought to be placed (with caution) in his fellow man, he did not long for faith. He did not long at all. Or he did but did not know it. And then, while he was longing without being aware that he longed, Gracie came to him. In the cool of an evening. Almost as if she'd been sent. As if someone knew it was not good for man to be alone.

PART TWO

1

HOWEVER FOOLISH IT SOUNDED, even to his own ears, whenever Jess said it out loud, it was true. Meeting Gracie was like a dream, the kind of dream you tried your best not to wake from, after all your haunted, fitful nights.

How unreal it had all seemed.

How mistrustful of the goodness he had been.

It was, after all, a high school dance. And he had arrived out of sorts.

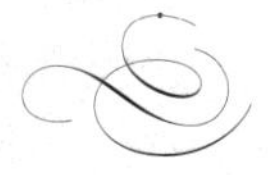

Jess had always disliked crowds, especially young ones, where ill-mannered stares multiplied like rabbits. Cows and horses, whose company he would take any day over that of a high-schooler, had no measuring sticks. They couldn't tell a giant from a dwarf. Also, he did not dance, and never had. He had to admit, though, that he was mostly sore at Mike Latona for what Jess felt was cheating, playing Rose Marie as his trump card.

Jess had a soft spot for Mike's younger sister, felt inexplicably tender toward her. From the first time he'd seen her, as a baby just three days old, and had been allowed to hold her in his arms, he had taken to Rose Marie as if she were his own small kin. And when in the year they turned thirteen, Mike got a temporary mean streak, during which he was either ignoring Rose Marie or teasing her unmercifully, Jess felt as if it were his own the hurt that showed in her quick black eyes. Eager to see their snap return, he had, on different occasions, taught her to make a grass blade whistle, to test out a grapevine before swinging on it, and to feel with her fingers in its mouth how hard a calf can suck. He had even, once, when her brother's meanness had been enough to make her cry, sat her across Jake's wide, patient old back for a quarter hour, which had pleased her so much it not only halted her tears but kept her from tattling on Mike.

Rose Marie was grown now, or very nearly, but Jess still loved her like a sister, so when Mike said their father would not let Rose Marie go to the Knights of Columbus dance without a chaperone, and that he would not chaperone unless Jess came along, he had no choice but to agree to go, of course, but he was sore.

And they were late. Mike's thirsty old Packard had run out of gas, so they'd had to walk half a mile to Latona's Deli to get his father's gas can and then the two blocks to the filling station and another half mile back to the car. They'd had to return the gas can to the deli too, because that was the only way Pop would let them take it in the first place.

"You'd think he'd be more grateful," Mike grumbled, between breaths, trotting to keep up with Jess's long stride as they were hustling from the deli back to his car. "We coulda left it at the curb."

Jess didn't bother to reply. He had known Mike a long time. If there was a deficit of gratitude in the family, he knew it was not Pop Latona who was lacking.

Inside the social hall, Jess stood awkwardly. He yanked at his tie and jerked at the sleeves of his coat, trying in vain to cover three inches of exposed bony wrist. He could not recall when he had last worn the suit. He only knew it had to have been before his last unwelcome spurt of growth, and that had been a little more than five years ago, just after his eighteenth birthday. Then it came to him. It was the funeral. A double funeral, it had been, so he had only needed it once. He scowled into the coatrack mirror, tossing back the rope of black hair he had pessimistically slathered with pomade, knowing at the time it would never stay put. Stooping to study his full reflection, he lost all hope of blending into the background. He glared, and the hayseed beanpole he saw in the glass glared back. He opened his jacket. There were half-moon stains under both arms. "What's the matter, Jesse?" he could almost hear his mother asking, in her soft drawl, as she laid a cool hand on his neck, combing the hair at his nape with her fingers, the way she had always done when he got anxious. "Land, son," she would say, lifting the damp strands, "you're perspiring like a sinner at altar call."

Jess edged toward the door. "I'll be in the car."

"Oh, no you don't." Mike moved as if to block his exit, and Jess couldn't help smiling. Mike stood five foot three with lifts in his shoes, and had to tilt his head back just to look Jess in the eye. "You're not going anywhere," Mike said, taking Jess by the coat sleeve, holding on to it while he glanced around the dance floor.

Balloons and crepe-paper streamers obscured the action. But Mike's eyes, almost as dark and shiny as his well-oiled hair, skimmed the hall with determination, searching for Rose Marie. He was doing a good deed, or so he seemed to think, by chaperoning her. But Jess knew the way his friend operated. Mike wasn't one for laying up treasures. He intended to get something more of an earthly nature for his troubles, and the sooner he found his kid sister and then ditched her, the sooner he could start reaping his reward.

The song was a popular one, judging by the crowd jamming the dance floor, but it came as no surprise to Jess that he'd never heard it. He got out very little. And the transistor radio in the barn had been hanging from a nail, silent as a stone, since the day Walter left. The song ground to a jerky halt then and the musicians, natty in slim suits and even slimmer ties, announced a break. During the interval, couples drifted over to the refreshment tables lining the walls, which opened the dance floor a little. Jess yawned. He looked at his watch.

Then, like a nut-brown sprite conjured to relieve his boredom, Rose Marie appeared at his elbow in a swirl of scarlet, her arm around a thin, light-haired girl in pale green. The girl looked as regretful as Jess felt. Rose Marie flashed Jess a quick, sweet smile then turned to her brother with brown eyes snapping. She punched him on the arm, hard.

"Some chaperone. The dance is half over. I could have met a fella and run off to Reno with him by now."

Mike grinned, rubbing his bicep. "You ain't been too lucky that way so far. Anyhow, don't work up a sweat. We're here now, ain't we?"

He went back to scanning the room, only now he was looking for unescorted girls. His gaze lighted on a girl seated by herself on a chair against the far wall then, and he was gone, lost immediately in the crowd. A few seconds later he reappeared on the dance floor, cheek to cheek with the girl, the later willingness he hoped to inspire already showing in her grateful expression. Rose Marie rolled her eyes and turned to Jess.

"Jess Hazel," she said, "I'd like you to meet my new best friend, Galina Morozov. Everyone calls her Gracie. Dance with her, and you'll soon see why."

Jess said, "Pleased," though he wasn't pleased at all, only felt more than ever like a sideshow freak. But he did force himself to look her in the eyes, bent his knees a little, and held out his hand. She took it, gazing right into his face. Her eyes were a shock, like none Jess had ever seen—whites of the purest white, the irises a deep warm gold. She held his gaze with an attitude so direct, so grave, it struck him deeper than any flirtatious gesture could have done. Then she smiled, and Jess felt a sudden peculiar ease, as if he had been journeying a long while and had just come in sight of the lit windows of home. How long he stood there, holding her hand and warming himself by the kind heat of that smile, he did not know. The band ended one song and began another, couples linked up, and still they stood, until a boy with a square jaw and a blond crew cut came and asked Rose Marie to dance.

"You don't mind if I dance with Skip?" Rose Marie asked, over her shoulder, though whether Gracie did mind hardly mattered because Rose Marie had already swung away, leaving her words to float on the air behind her.

In a mute, stiff-jointed attempt at gallantry, Jess offered Gracie a chair. And when she was seated, he took the one next to her, nervously shifting his rangy length to fit the narrow space between rows. His legs had always been in the way unless he was standing on them. There were a few ways to cope. He could sit sideways on a chair, legs crossed, or he could slump and stow the fool things like oars under the seat in front of him. But he worried that crossed legs would seem girlish and slumping disrespectful, so he made a tent of his knees and rested his feet flat on the floor. He looked over at Gracie. She was watching, her face expressionless, an oval of calm. His own cheeks buzzed with heat, and he knew they had to be a bright red about now, declaring his discomfort. She bent her head and began rummaging through her little beaded clasp-bag, giving him time to gather his wits.

Mousy. He was amazed at the way Mike had chosen to describe the Russki friend they would be chaperoning along with Rose Marie. Lord, he could not think of a description more unfit. Why, even in the dim light of the gymnasium, her hair shone like sunlight slanting through a jar of maple syrup. He watched, transfixed, as swallow-tail hands suddenly floated up to tuck a strand back into its pin. And scrawny? Jess wanted to laugh. He only wished himself more rounded in his reading, for there was surely some epic poem in which a slenderness like hers was described. Their eyes met, and he marveled at hers all over again, wondered why Mike had not mentioned them. They were remarkable, really, those lantern-lit eyes, the color of antique gold. He cleared his throat.

"I can't ask you to dance."

She raised her eyebrows, a movement so slight it was almost imperceptible.

"Not that I wouldn't like to," Jess said, quickly. "It's just that I'm generally either milking a cow or getting ready to. Not a lot of time in between there for dancing lessons. I've just never learned."

She looked amused, the corners of her mouth twitching. Jess began to despair. He was unexpectedly drawn to this strange, lovely girl, so plain-faced and uncontrived, and longed as he never had to be someone other than he was: a man whose tongue went lame when he most needed it to work. "You must think I have awful manners," he said.

"Oh, manners," she said, waving her hand. "If you're lacking there, please don't worry. My father says good manners are like priest's cassocks." She thickened her accent then as she spoke, lowering her voice to imitate a deep, gruff bass, "'Beware, Galya,' he says, 'for much evil and ugliness may be hiding underneath.' Of course," she laughed, "he is only paraphrasing Gogol, but I don't tell him I know that. He's a good papa and deserves to be wise." She looked out to the dance floor then and gave a small shrug. "Pretty silly sort of dance anyway, don't you think?

"What is?"

"The jitterbug."

He liked the way she pronounced the word *jitterbug*. Liked the way she stressed the *t*'s and rolled the *r* in her light and easy voice.

"Huh," he said, relaxing a little. "So that's what it's called." He looked around the gym floor stacked with couples. Heads jerked and arms flailed. "Puts me in mind of a hen fight."

She laughed.

Then, just to keep her talking, he asked, "Is there a dance you don't think is silly?"

"Of course. A waltz isn't."

"I don't know a lot about it. But I'm pretty sure they're not going to play a waltz."

"I'm sure you're right. And that's why I usually don't come to these things. Don't look so worried." She patted his shoulder. No more than a friendly gesture, just a light brush of her hand, but Jess felt the heat of blood rushing to his face all over again. "I'm just fine sitting out," she added, quickly, seeing his face. "To be perfectly honest, I don't even feel like dancing." She laughed again, a bright, birdsong sound from high in her throat. "You don't know how, and I don't want to. Seems to me we ought to get along just fine."

They both laughed then, and this time when their eyes met, Jess saw that hers had changed. They were darker now, almost glowed, making him think of a fire at dusk.

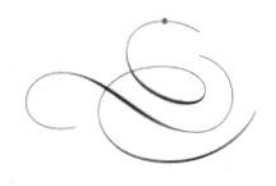

Gracie was right. They did get along. Just fine. It wasn't until he was back at home, late that night, that Jess realized they had spent the entire evening sitting on hardwood-slatted folding chairs talking. And, as he remarked to Becky the next morning before he turned her out to graze, it was the craziest thing, but he couldn't recall a smidgen of the conversation, so intoxicated had he been by Gracie's amber eyes, her swooshing consonants and tilted vowels. "Couldn't have been any drunker," he said, "if some joker had doctored the punch."

2

Kerry Mountain
May 1, 1957

THAT SPRING WHEN THE SWALLOWS came back to Kerry Mountain, as they did every spring, as they had done since long before the mountain had a name, they found Tsura growing up, growing tall.

It was the first day of May. Eli stood at the bottom of the stairs, gazing through the doorway into the kitchen, watching her move quietly about the room, thinking that his time with her had passed up to now in a way that did not have much to do with months or years. Seasons came and went. The snow fell. The wind blew. The creek flowed. The birds sang. The sun shone. Aside from this day, the day of Tsura's dawning, as Pat called that so-bright morning of her birth here on the peak, there had been little need to measure it any other way.

"Wiselike," Pat had also said, on the day she was born, and almost any day he had seen her since. And it was true. Her wide, dark eyes shined with something so old and odd it often worried Eli. Why it did, what it was he feared, he did not try to know. He would rather worry and let her be as she was than to know and act in some other way because of knowing.

She was taller than usual for a little girl of five, he thought, watching her rise on tiptoe to fetch her tin cup down from the shelf and pump herself a drink. But maybe not. It had been too long since he was around his own little sisters. Also, he was short, and that made him a bad judge. It could be that her thin little legs only made her seem tall. Long as a pair of willow switches they were. That is what Pat said. Attached to her feet by sparrow's ankles. He also claimed that angel's hands had whittled her face, scooped the cleft in her chin, sunk the hollows in her cheeks. Such fancy speech. Pat never worried that his words were vain or unnatural. For a quiet man, he had never been slow to speak on the mountain. But this was all right with Eli. He had even come to welcome the old man's talk. It made him to know that what was blown about in his own head when a storm was brewing might not be so crazy as he thought. He had no gift like Pat's for speaking what was in his mind, but what they saw when looking at Tsura was the same. As to what to do about it, he was not sure. For now, it did not matter. They would go on as they had been. But he could not help wishing she could stay a child. A child does not mind that she is beautiful.

Just now she was puttering about the kitchen, sweeping the floor with a tiny straw broom he had made as a gift for her birthday. Always curious, alert to the smallest happenings, she had spied a small black beetle among the crumbs and stopped to watch it creep. It was not her way to molest the insect. When it turned, changed direction, and began climbing her bare big toe, she kept very still, waiting until it was safe on the other side before she went back to her sweeping.

The farrier would come this morning, Eli decided. Pat's visits were not regular. He came whenever he wished. But always on the first day of May. Eli had no more finished the thought when Tsura stopped sweeping and looked expectantly toward the door. A moment later, there came a knock. He nodded, telling her to go. She dropped her broom and ran to open it.

Pat stood, as he always did, looking around surprised, as if the door had opened of its own accord. Tsura knew the game well. She stood on his boots and raised her hands, waiting to be swung up to his shoulder where she began to fish in his shirt pocket for a stick of gum.

"I have a present," she said solemnly, pointing to her broom. "It's my birthday."

"What?" Pat opened his blue eyes wide, as if in shock. "A spring peeper with a birthday all her own? Never heard of such a thing. All the ones I'm acquainted with celebrate their birthdays together."

"Why?" Tsura asked.

"Well," Pat said, "because none of 'em knows for sure which day they hatched. Which is why they throw a party every night of spring. What a ruckus!"

"Do they get presents?" Tsura asked, wide-eyed now herself.

"Well, not near so fine as you've got there," Pat said. "They have little need for brooms, you see. But they get presents of such things as frogs long for. I guess you've never heard them sing of mud cakes and shoo-fly pies."

Tsura shook her head, looking suddenly dejected that she had never heard a tree frog sing a birthday song.

"Well," Pat said, quickly, "count your blessings, child." He swung her in a gentle arc to the floor. "As I said, it's a mighty joyful noise. But an awful ruckus."

Eli saw the sideways glance, Pat avoiding his gaze. Pat knew, because Eli had told him, that Amish children received only the plainest truth about the world and the God who made it for their use. Pat thought it a very fine way of teaching children, he said, but Eli doubted it. Pat, at least, never followed the rule. He said it was his father's fault because the Badgers had once all been peddlers. It was an unreliable trade, and in all the long, wandering hours, a peddler would spin yarns to keep the next farmwife considering his wares while she listened. If the story was amusing enough, she was put in a better mood to purchase. When it came to telling tales, he had once said, in defense of some fib he had told Tsura, even a half Badger couldn't help himself. Eli never let on to Pat, but he wouldn't have put his foot down about the storytelling anyway. It wouldn't be right to ask Pat to bend to Amish ways when he himself, who had been born to them, couldn't.

There was not much of the Amish daughter in Tsura. To be sure of this, Eli had kept the image of his youngest sister, Ruth, always in his mind as he tended to Tsura's needs, for the two girls were no more alike than a dragonfly and an ant. Ruth was born in the long shadow of womanhood, of sisterhood. The good hand of duty rocked the Amish girl's cradle. Tsura's obedience was to something other, something Eli could not see or understand. He only knew that it seemed to bid her to tender, gentle acts, and he tried to leave her free to follow. If his mother would be scandalized to see this girl he was raising, all bare of head, thick, dark curls like a wild cane of blackberries vining down her little back and around her shoulders, well, so be it. It would not be the first time Eli Zook had been the cause of scandal.

There was a loud thump, suddenly, that brought Eli's thoughts back to what was happening in the kitchen. The sound had been Pat, stomping his boot against the hard plank floor. Tsura, who was kneeling on the floor, had stopped intently unwrapping the stick of gum she had found in his pocket and was staring up at Pat, dark eyes wide.

"Tsura," he said, clapping a hand to his forehead, "we plumb forgot it's May Day!" He looked at his watch. "Half-past basket time too. Don't you think you'd better go to the front porch and have a look around?"

A loud squeaking of hinges answered his question. The next sound was that of the screen door shutting with a bang. Tsura was gone.

Pat turned. As always, his look was searching. His blue gaze swept Eli head to toe and then moved about the room seeking signs that all was well, and would be well, until he could visit the peak again. Though it pained Eli, he endured with patience. Theirs was a good contract. A handshake agreement. And that look of Pat's was in it.

"There's school to think about this fall," Pat said. "I guess you've considered it."

"Yah. I have."

"Will you send her?"

"Nah."

"I thought not."

They sat without speaking after that. A great deal was said, though, in the silence. Eli explained without words that sending Tsura to school would be akin to shoeing and harnessing one of those wild marsh island ponies Pat always said she reminded him of, the ones that ran about free along the eastern coast. All horses are not born to plow, you know, he said. Yes, Pat agreed, and remarked that the knowledge she already owned would likely be lost on the finest of classroom teachers, anyhow. She was gifted, no doubt, very keen. But her keenness was not of the sort that could be tested or measured in numbers against a mean. Her spirit is made of the same stuff as moth's wings, strong in flight but easy to crush in the hand. It will be up to you and me, my friend, Pat said, to keep it from injury.

Eli made a pot of coffee, and they shared it cup by cup, mostly in the same silence. When the coffee was gone, Pat rose from the table.

"She'll have found the basket by now, I reckon. The violets."

"Yah, the violets," Eli said, his bare lip twitching with the hint of a smile. "And the sweets."

Pat grinned, impenitent.

"And the sweets."

3

Hazel Valley
July 1957

THREE MONTHS AFTER MEETING Gracie Morozov at the dance, Jess was no less stricken. Like a spindly, determined sapling, love had taken strong and rapid root—despite, he always said later, the rocky barrenness of the ground.

Volunteer love.

So unlooked for, and yet so insistent.

What could a man do?

Jess had only one answer: Let it grow. Tend to it. Cultivate it. Help it along. But let it grow.

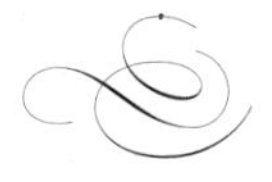

In the dining room his mother had kept a hutch that had a hidden drawer, a place for hiding small valuables. Once Jess had decided, had determined, that he would allow himself to love Gracie in earnest, he rummaged around in it, hunting a certain family heirloom. It was a painful task, for what Millie held dear no thief would consider stealing. Among the things he lifted out and set aside were a crumbling, string-tied packet of Valentine messages his aunts and grandmother had sent across the miles to keep strong the memory of their love; an ivory box, rattling with Jess and Walter's baby teeth; and a miniature bonnet of tatted lace, made for a baby girl who was born too soon to need it. There was also a snapshot that caused him to feel the heat of recollected shame, for it was of Walter at two, sitting on the floor next to the Hazel family cradle, rocking a swaddled Jess. As a child Jess had got the idea from the photo that human babies (he knew by age nine, of course, how animals managed it) emerged from cocoons like moths. It was a notion he liked a lot and held fast to for longer than he should have. So long that his ignorance became an embarrassment to Walter, who in the frankest of brotherly speeches, given one day as they were riding the bus home from school, finally rid Jess of it.

The photograph went into the pile, pitifully small, when you considered all it stood for, and Jess went back to rummaging. At last, tucked way back, behind a stack of yellowed envelopes (letters addressed to a Miss Mildred Jenkins at Slippery Rock State Teacher's College in Clyde's narrow, backward-slanting hand), he found what he'd been seeking. The ring. The one his father had given his mother on the day of their engagement, the story of which involved a character unfamiliar to Jess. In it, a reckless, lovesick young Clyde risked an ill-looking winter sky and went sliding over ice-covered hills and rivers to land (on one knee, the story went) in the borough of Slippery Rock. Millie always said she was pleased to accept the ring, insisting that she had worn it all that year at school with a great deal of pride. But when her wedding day had passed, she did as all the Hazel wives before her had done and placed it dutifully back in its green velvet box. Much too fine an adornment, it was generally agreed, for the hand of a dairy farmer's wife.

From time to time, Jess remembered, Millie would take the ring out for her boys to admire, slipping it onto her finger, turning it this way and that, so they could see it wink and shine. But when they tried to touch it, she'd wave their hands away, clutching it to her thin little chest, trying in her soft, shy way to be stern.

"It's not mine to let you handle," she'd say. "I'm only keeping it for Walter's wife."

"Millie, you're a sensible woman," their father would remark, as she returned the ring to its box. But Jess had seen his mother's face. She never looked sensible to him, slipping the box back into the drawer, stowing it away out of sight. She looked wistful.

It was not fancy, the ring. The diamond in it was so small as to be insignificant, and the pearl could hardly be called perfect. But it was made of good gold. It was part of a set too, though Gracie would never own its companion. That was a plain, slim band Millie never took off and was, in fact, wearing still. Of that Jess had made sure, and was never sorry he had, for as it turned out, the ring was to be the only familiar thing about her as she lay in repose. The Jenkins aunts had supplied a portrait from Millie's youth, her sepia lips and cheeks retouched in an unnatural shade of pink, and the mortician had done his best to copy it. The sister the Jenkins aunts remembered, though, and the woman the neighbors came to view at calling hours, bore scant resemblance to Jess's mother.

"So pretty yet. And nearly forty-five."

This is what they all said, gazing into her casket.

But it was Millie at the last Jess kept in his mind, for it somehow eased his hurt. The mournful shade of her dark eyes. The small straight spine, bent as an old woman's with weariness and fret. Millie had a few friends in Prospect, a couple of acquaintances in Rose Point, people she could count on in a pinch, but not one that could be called close. She was, after all, not the sort of woman who took pleasure in cake walks or church bazaars. She disliked gossip, even the harmless sort, and kept mostly to herself. If those who glanced down at her pale painted corpse and said such kind, foolish things knew little of her burden, Jess could hardly resent their lack. How much, after all, had he really known? How much had Clyde?

Jess took the ring to a jeweler in Pittsburgh, who put a glass to his eye and inspected it, pronouncing it sound enough for the purpose. And the next day—it was a clear, hot Sunday morning in July—after the cows were milked and turned out to graze, he showered and went into town, to Latona's Deli. The store was locked and dark, of course, so he went around back as he had done as a boy, climbed the stairs, and rang the bell. Rita came, dressed for church, opened the door, and peered out. She had a spatula in her hand and black-bristled rollers in her silvery dark hair. She peered at Jess, then shook her head, opening the door wide.

"My God, Jesse," she said coolly, standing aside to let him pass, "I almost don't know you. Such a long time, and you so skinny. Like a flagpole. Don't you eat?"

In reply Jess only smiled, marveling, as he had always done when entering the Latona's apartment, that it had somehow nested nine children within its walls. As a guest, he had always liked the chaos, the constant shrill of Rita—who minded the clutter something terrible and yelled and scolded constantly to prevent its overgrowth. And he had envied also, especially once Walter was gone, the closeness, both physical and emotional, of the siblings, who scraped and squabbled as fondly as a pack of dogs. He was hardly inside when she pushed him into a chair at the kitchen table, setting before him a plate of sausage and eggs, scrambled with red peppers, potatoes, and onions.

"So," she said, hand on her hip, "what's up?"

"I've come to ask you to make me a picnic," Jess said, shoveling the eggs into his mouth. They were surely meant for Pop, but he was suddenly hungry, realizing it must be after eight o'clock, and he had been so eager to get to town he had forgotten to eat breakfast.

"A picnic?" Rita's gaze was sharp now. She was the same woman of Jess's boyhood, aloof and bossy-tongued as a barn cat, and just as helplessly curious.

"Yep," he said, "a picnic. I'll pay, of course."

"You want hoagies?"

"No hoagies. A spread. Chipped ham, salami, kolbassy. Cheese. Olives. Pickled stuff. And whatever else your Russian customers buy."

"Russian, huh? Ah, I got it. The special picnic."

She left the room then and came back after a little while dressed in everyday clothes, tying on her shop apron, looking pleased with herself.

"You gonna marry that girl."

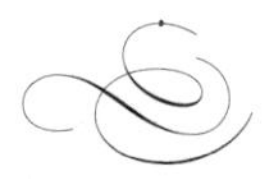

That afternoon Jess and Gracie walked out to the old orchard with the sun at their backs, carrying a basket packed with Rita's picnic. They followed the sled path, bees buzzing about their heads as they passed the hives, Jess easing off the path to pick a fistful of poppies, returning to hand them to her as they walked, ducking her into the woods once to show her a walking fern, and while he had her there in the dusky shadow of the trees, stealing a kiss, as if they were a courting couple of old, all the while feeling smug over his picnic idea, for he would already be on his knees, that way, when he asked.

She accepted.

Instantly.

With eyes lit gold. As if only to increase his wonder at such an upstart, insistent love.

He was overjoyed, of course. Yet he was also dismayed, even a little frightened, for he knew it was only fair to tell her the truth about himself before letting her decide.

There was this Light, you see.

When it came down to actually saying it, though, he didn't. He found that he could not tell her the truth about himself at all. Not the whole of it, anyway. He lay back, stretching himself out on the blanket—one of Millie's crazy quilts, found in her cedar chest—the lower part of his legs buried in the grass, and fixing his gaze on the sky, said instead that there were a few things she might want to consider before accepting to wed a dairy farmer.

She was sitting next to him on the quilt at the time, examining the ring. It was a fine fit. He had been surprised, in fact, at how slim her fingers were, how easily it had gone on, once he'd worked it gently past her knuckle. (As slim as Millie's had been, evidently, for the ring would not need to be sized.)

"Like what?" she said.

"Like it's not all this." Jess waved his hand in the air, making it walk back the way they had come to the orchard. "All hay and honey and wildflowers."

"Well, I know that already," she said, and a shade of something came into her voice that Jess would learn to know well. A bristling. The only warning he would ever get, along with a yellow flash of her eyes, that she was offended and about to set him straight. "You are forgetting we were farmers once," she said. "Or, Mama and Papa were. I was only a little girl. But I recall the smell, and the sorrows, of a barnyard, if that's what you mean. What else?"

"Money."

"Money."

Jess kept his eyes on the sky, on the one tiny cloud left in it, now shaping itself into a baby's fist, dimples and all. If insecurity was to begin flickering now in her eyes, he couldn't bear to see it.

"Yes, money," he said. "It's scarce. And getting scarcer. Farming is just about one of the worst jobs you can have these days. And farms of our kind, well . . . you should probably marry a salesman, or a lawyer. Or better yet, get to be one yourself."

"I don't care about money."

"You might, when there's none around."

At that, Gracie got quiet. She turned her own gaze to the sky, while Jess lay in the grip of dread, working to keep his limbs still. They were goading him to leap up and run. In the end, she only shrugged.

"You've got a lot to learn about me," she said.

And that was all.

It was a promise, though. Jess could hear it in her voice.

He might have been a dead man she'd stumbled on, lying in the orchard grass, the way she sank to her knees beside him then, and put her hand over his eyes, closing them both at once. Her lips were so, so soft as they landed, barely grazing the skin of his eyelids. Jess trembled and sighed out loud, sick with relief. He had somehow found the girl (or had she found him?) who could love a husk.

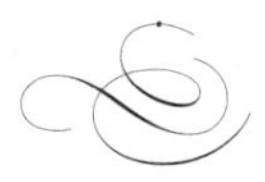

Early the next morning, the telephone rang.

It was Gracie.

"How do you feel about the Orthodox Church?"

"Why do you ask?"

"Our marriage hinges on it."

Jess was stunned. Very quickly he decided this must be her idea of a joke. Just as quickly, he knew that it wasn't. There had been no hint of humor in her voice. And suddenly he was irritated.

"How do I feel about the Orthodox Church? I don't know a thing about it! That's how I feel. How do you feel about the Presbyterian Church?"

"Are you Presbyterian?"

"No."

Gracie sighed. "If you want to marry me, Jess, it will have to be in my church. You must understand how important this is. And not just to me, to my parents. You know I'm all they have."

She decreed this with such bravery, the way Jess had imagined telling her about the Light. And he had no doubt she meant it, every word. For if there was anything he knew about Gracie Morozov after three months of loving her, it was that she was serious about God. It wasn't a thing she talked about endlessly like some religious girls Jess had known—she seemed to take her faith as a natural gift, much as she did the shine and gloss of her hair or the unusual hue of her eyes, and rarely spoke of it directly, but he would have to be a fool not to see how it affected everything she said and did. They had never even been on a real date until the picnic in the orchard. All their evenings had been spent sitting on her porch, the curtains not even drawn on the front room window. One thing was sure, though, he wasn't about to take back his proposal. Not marry Gracie. The thought panicked him. He could more easily give up air now, stop breathing in and out. The Hazels had once all been Quakers, but that was generations back. And though Jess had sometimes thought it would have made things a good deal easier, and wished like everything they had, Clyde and Millie had left him no religion to call his own. He saw no other way but to agree to Gracie's terms and accepted to be baptized. To the voice, so still and small, that urged him to consider the cavern in his chest, he turned a deaf ear. Gracie believed in one God, the Father Almighty. He believed in Gracie. That, he reasoned, would be faith enough.

Of course, he was not fitting into the font at Holy Transfiguration Church. And so it was that at the age of twenty-three, Jess joined the Christian fold standing on ancestral land, for it was into the waters of Muddy Creek that Father Antony took him by the hand and brought him—Jess floating on his back like a felled pine, the creek trying to carry him downstream, the priest calmly retrieving him, taking him three times under. Once for the Father. Once for the Son. Once for the Holy Spirit.

4

THEY WERE MARRIED on a Sunday in early November. The hills were iced in the first white snow, the trees in the churchyard draped in it, as if in fine, hand-worked lace, and Gracie was so luminous in a long-sleeved gown of cream-white silk, so serene as Father Antony took their hands, linking them together for life (The child of God, Galina, is wed to the child of God, Jesse), so plainly honest (Have you promised yourself to any other man? I have not, Reverend Father), Jess nearly wept.

There were no pews.

No spectators posing as guests.

Mike and Rose Marie were there, and Peggy Badger, without Pat, who stayed out on the lawn, wishing his very best to all who walked past, stomping his feet to keep warm, and regretfully declining all invitations to come into the church. Inside, the guests were stacked about the nave like firewood all cut and stored for the winter. Jess and Gracie, holding lit candles—beeswax, to show the purity of their prayer, and of their hearts' intentions—stood in the center of them, surrounded, upheld, by all the hope, all the goodwill.

It was cold outside, though not bitterly, yet very hot in the church, what with all the oil lamps lit and burning before all the grave, dark eyes of saints, and the press of guests crowded in so close, their faces fairly lit and shining, radiating their warmth. More than once during the long, mysterious ceremony, Jess felt his knees buckle.

He felt so faint, in fact, that when Father Antony finally took up the crowns, a small, low groan escaped his lips, causing Gracie's mama to cast him a sharp look. It was a sound of relief, though, and that was all, for at last he understood something of what was happening and knew that it was almost over. Gracie had explained this portion of the ceremony in detail:

"You'll be crowned," she'd said.

"Wait," Jess had said, "Hold up a minute. Are you telling me this involves a blow to the head?"

"You might feel as if that's what happened, by the time it's over," she said, smiling, indulging him, despite her general seriousness toward anything to do with the wedding, in the corniness of his joke. "We wear crowns. Like royalty. Only our crowns will only look like gold, and the jewels will be made of colored glass. And you will feel ridiculous. But that's all right, because the crowns are only there to show that marriage makes us martyrs, in a way."

"Martyrs," Jess said. "You and me."

"Yes," Gracie said.

"That's awfully morbid, don't you think? You Russians sure take a funny view of things."

"I don't think it's funny at all," Gracie said, all soberness now. "Or morbid either. Vechnaya Pamyat, I say. Memory Eternal to the self-centered Galina Morozov. I die for you. You die for me. And together, we live. Don't you think that's the most beautiful, hopeful thing you've ever heard?"

"I think it sounds plain crazy," Jess had said, softly. She was so grave, so in earnest. He fought the urge to take her full in his arms right then, to feel all her good warmth, not just that of her smile or her eyes. She promised such sweetness. He had known such bitterness. But he had agreed to her terms. No loving of that kind until the honeymoon. Jess shook his head, as much to clear it, keep it from getting ahead of itself, as to demonstrate his point. "Where's my crown?" he said. "I'm all in."

He was too.

Jesse Hazel was all in.

PART THREE

1

Hazel Valley
October 18, 1969

ON A COLD, WET FALL DAY, Jess sat at the kitchen table, staring at a page he had torn from the calendar weeks ago and for some reason had not thrown away. September was old news. It was well into October, half the month already gone. Soon enough the year would be gone also. A year that, in the proper way of things, had been of staggering importance to some folks in the world and unremarked by others. Who in Vietnam, for instance, could care that the waters of Muddy Creek were soon to be impounded to form a lake? A place for city folks to fish and swim and run the motors off their speedboats. He crumpled the calendar page into a ball, took aim, and threw it across the kitchen, where it landed on the floor beside the wastebasket. He looked over at Gracie. She hadn't moved, stood as still and quiet as she had all morning, gazing out the backdoor window. Watching the rain.

Come the tenth of next month, they would mark twelve years together. Of which all but the first two (slow and sweet) had shot by at a speed he couldn't fathom. For a dozen years, he'd been loving Gracie, and he was still in wonderment over the fact, though here he sat, with his elbows on the table, in the kitchen she had made her own, filling it with sights and smells and sounds wonderfully strange to Jess, and surely all the more to his ghosts.

She ate salted fish and pickled pork fat. She fermented bread to make a drink she called kvass (fermented everything, it seemed to

Jess). She lit beeswax candles and oil lamps to pray, hung the lamps from gilded chains to swing and sway before icons—images of her sober saints painted on scraps of wood—paying them curious devotion. She liked American music, especially jazz, and played it loud from the speakers of the hi-fi stereo cabinet that was a wedding gift from her parents, Ivan and Darya. She had her own way, too, of running what she claimed as her portion of the farm, which consisted, the best Jess could figure, of the house, the garden, and a coop full of uppity, pure-bred hens. Particular about the cleanliness of her house, she'd let go the two women Jess had finally got to come on opposite Mondays every week to clean the floors and do his washing. Opal first, then Liz.

Jess had been a little sorry over Opal, for she was a kind woman and like Margit Busco had insisted on cooking for Jess, leaving the freezer full of casseroles he could thaw and reheat. She was some sort of eldress in her church, though, and Jess had to admit, when Gracie complained, that she did preach Jesus to anyone who happened into the house. He had in truth mostly avoided her, leaving her pay on the kitchen table and keeping to the barn until he saw the taillights of her big Buick as she pulled away down the lane.

Liz was a McKee, descended of the McKees who were one of the first white families to settle the borough, and married to a Christie, another large old settling family. The girl was quiet enough—no sermons—but lazy. When she wasn't standing on the porch smoking cigarettes and staring moon-eyed at Jess as he went about his work, she was swabbing the floors with dirty mop water, leaving stains along edges of the living room rugs. Gracie had little patience for the preaching, and none for the sloth. How she had let both women down so carefully, each convinced that leaving the job was her own idea, was still a puzzle to Jess. But then, it was just that way with his wife.

Jess sipped at his coffee. His wife! How much he still savored those words. She had lifted the curtain aside (gone was the faded, soot-stained gingham of Jess's childhood; her windows were hung in plain white linen, crisp and clean) to better see the rain. It ran zigzag down the window, like an old woman's tears. He was reminded of his mother, for weather like this had always set Millie brooding. "A rain in autumn is a melancholy guest," she used to say, her gaze mournfully darkened, chin cradled in her small hand. And because he had passed many a dreary fall day cooped up inside when he wanted to be digging fence holes or mending tack or plowing a field, Jess had always thought his mother had spoken right. Gracie, though, did not agree. She was fond of rain, whatever the season.

Peculiar fond, he had sometimes thought, when they first married, watching her rush into the house at the first glimpse of a darkening sky to hustle her begonias out onto the front step. She would stand under the roof of the porch then, content as a garden toad, to watch it coming down. And in weather too harsh for porches and flowers, he would often find her wedged into a corner of the divan, the curtains opened wide to the storm, peacefully knitting. Most often she would be working a skein of yarn into mittens for one of Rose Marie's older children or fashioning a sweater for the newest baby. Sometimes, though, it was a pair of thick warm socks for him. Jess liked to hear the noise her needles made, their pleasant tap, tap, tap, keeping quiet rhythm with the rain.

This was not to be that kind of morning. He guessed the rain on the roof today must sound to her ears like small, pattering feet. And there would be no tucking into a cozy corner and knitting—a tiny sweater would be her undoing. It had been more than an hour, and he had not seen her venture beyond the kitchen window.

"There goes my apple-picking," she said.

She turned from the window to face him, hands folded over her chest, eyebrows knit into a taut line across her forehead.

"Well, it's just a trip out to the orchard," he replied. "Nobody called off a wedding."

As soon as he spoke, he regretted it. He had not meant to sound so brusque. What he had hoped was to see her smile. He hitched his chair closer to the table and slumped over his coffee cup, watching her from the corner of his eye. She acted as if she hadn't heard, turning to the window again and pressing her nose against the glass. She tapped with one finger a patch of lighter gray no bigger than a cat's foot and barely visible under the top of the frame.

"You know, I think it will quit soon, from the looks of it over there."

"Can't store wet apples," Jess warned, in a gentler voice. He slipped the plastic sleeve from his newspaper and twisted off the rubber band, dropping it into the jar next to the salt shaker. "Better wait until tomorrow."

"Tomorrow is Sunday," she said.

"Well, then, the minute you get home from the service, I'll take you down there myself. In the pickup."

"There won't be a need for that," she said, her back still to him. "The sled track is packed hard as paved road. A day's rain won't muddy it. If it's going to be tomorrow afternoon, Mama will probably want to come with me, and her car has those big tires. It will do fine."

She sighed again, peering closer at the patch, as if willing it to widen. With eyes fixed on the sky, she reached down and unfastened the tail of the thick braid she had plaited her hair into before bed the night before. Slender fingers darted between the sections, freeing, combing, smoothing. Then, as quickly as she had undone the hair, she divided and plaited it again, jerking without mercy at the strands until the braid hung limp and obedient at her shoulder. A heaviness settled into Jess's own chest.

"Can't you be glad for the rain, Gracie?" he asked. "Old Elijah didn't beg the good Lord for it as hard as you have the last two months."

"Oh, I am," she said. "I am."

But Jess could plainly see that she was not. He put down his newspaper and took her by the hand. He pulled her to his chest and held her close. She pressed her cheek against the soft flannel of his shirt as if seeking comfort. But the muscles strung tight along her narrow back told his hands the truth. She was humoring him, letting him soothe her for his sake.

It wasn't the rain, laying down blankets of rusted yellow leaves and ruining her apple-picking that had dimmed the light in Gracie's eyes. Jess had watched her fumbling with her apron strings this morning, feeling blindly for each step as she came down the stairs. Yesterday she'd thought a baby might be on the way. Today she knew one wasn't. Handyman that he was, Jess could not fix shattered hope. He pulled on his boots, shrugged into his coat, drained his coffee cup, and escaped through the kitchen door. Rain pelted his head and shoulders all the way to the barn.

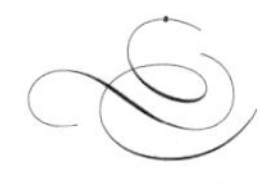

Becky nickered low as he ducked in. She turned her flanks to the rear of the stall and pressed her chest against the lower half door, stretching her neck toward Jess. Her nose softly quivered, wet nostrils flaring wide as she tried to catch his scent. In the gloom her black coat seemed dull, the color flat. No glints of mahogany shone through from underneath, as they did in direct sunlight. She lowered her head and rolled it sideways to observe Jess with a kind, dark eye.

"Mornin' girl."

Jess held his hand out, and she rested her chin in his palm, encouraging him to dig his fingertips into the stiff whorled slash of white between her eyes, to scratch the only place she couldn't find a way to reach. He obliged, and when he had finished scratching, she velveted his cheeks with her muzzle, mingling her warm breath with his. Her greeting, along with the heated, earthy odors stirred up by her hooves, cheered him considerably.

He went into the tack room and lifted a hoof pick from its nail, found a curry comb and a stiff brush, and scooped up a quarter can of oats. He led the big horse out of the stall, clipped a lead rope to her halter and tied it to the handle of the feed room door, then poured the oats into the bucket already hanging there. While she lipped the oats, he ran a hand down her foreleg, clicking his tongue as he reached the fetlock. She cocked her leg at the knee and lifted her hoof. He peeled out and flicked onto the barn floor a disc of manure-packed straw the size of a dinner plate. When each hoof had been cleaned, he turned his attention to her coat, running the curry comb over it in circular motions. All the while he listened to the rain pound the barn's tin roof, savoring the comfort a man could find in a mundane task.

Dread and hope had sat side by side in his chest the last few days. He was almost relieved the disappointment was here in front of them to deal with, the suspense done with for a time. For Gracie, he tried to keep faith, as she still did. But after ten years, and too many mornings like this one, he could not match her yearning. Truth be told, he never had. All he had ever longed for, all he had needed, he found in full measure in Gracie. Sure, her sorrow grieved him, but mostly for her sake. Mostly. No heir at all, and Hazel Valley would pass someday into the hands of strangers, folks who would either gather the fruit of his family's labor or disesteem it completely, leaving it to rot underfoot. If not for fear of that eventuality, Jess admitted (though only to himself, and once or twice, to Becky), he could be content to grow old with only Gracie. Together, though alone.

Near noon, Jess's stomach began to call for dinner. He stopped his work and headed for the house. As he reached the top of the hill, he saw the mail car circling through the drive. It was Pop Latona. Ever since the big new supermarket had opened in Ellwood City and started tempting away the deli's customers, Pop had been working half-time of a morning, sorting and then carrying the Rose Point mail. Rose Marie said the job had been a godsend. Pop was old-world, and the fickleness of his customers had just about done him in. Working for the US Postal Service, Pop didn't have to worry about anyone being fickle. Loyalty had nothing to do with it. Folks either had mail, or they didn't.

"Thought it was not a good idea, putting this in the box." Pop rolled his window down, just enough to slide an envelope out without letting the rain in. "That's the heavy paper," he said. "Maybe something important."

"Thanks, Pop," Jess said. While the old man watched, chewing anxiously on his mustache, Jess made a show of stowing the envelope away safe in his coat, slipping it into the dry inside pocket.

On the back porch, Jess took off his boots, stacking them as Millie had taught her boys to do, side by side on the mat. He stopped just inside the kitchen door, inhaling the good smell of the stew Gracie had made for supper the night before. She was setting a bowl on the table for him as he entered the kitchen. She took a chair across from Jess's, pulling her sweater so tight he could see the sharp points of her shoulder blades under the light wool fabric. Steam rose up from the bowls.

"Mmmm, boy," Jess said, brightly, "my belly was recalling this just now. Kept pokin' me to come on up here and see if you were serving leftovers."

She smiled. A thin, bare smile.

Jess spooned in a bite of the stew. It did taste fine. Gracie had a particular way with herbs and seasonings, and the flavors had honeymooned overnight, turning what had already been good into a savory reward. He lifted out a bay leaf and set it on the bowl flange, then busied himself with eating. But soon his own chewing and swallowing began to sound vulgar to his ears against her silence. Another time he would have enjoyed seconds. Now, when the last spoonful of stew was gone, he stood up.

"I believe I'll make a fire. Take off the chill."

"It is cold," she said, shivering. "Seems as though my bones need a sweater of their own. It would be wasteful, I suppose, to use the furnace so early in the season."

"Well," he said, "I would hate to use up coal on nothing but a rainy day. Never know this time of year when we could get a real cold snap, and there we'd be, short on fuel. A fire's nicer than furnace heat anyhow, don't you think? You can make yourself a cup of tea and sit up to the fireplace the way you do, with your feet on the hearth."

He took his soup bowl to the sink and ran water in it, gave it a swipe with the dish mop, and left it to soak. When he turned around again, he saw Gracie's hands clenched, her knuckles white, saw that her spoon rested clean and shiny on her folded napkin, and his chest tightened. He came over, and dried his hands on the towel still slung across her shoulder.

"I'll go down to the basement," he said, "and make sure the furnace is up to snuff. And if the fire doesn't do it for you, we'll have it on. Cost be damned. How's that?"

"No, don't do it," she said. "Now that you've mentioned it, a hot wood fire does sound nice."

She looked up at Jess then, meeting his gaze for the first time all day. Her lower lip trembled ever so slightly before she caught it with her teeth, and he saw the slenderness of the thread she had been trying not to break. He reached down and brought her to him, folding her into his arms, held her close and tight. He felt her give, shoulders jerking in silent spasms, tears soaking into his shirt.

"Jess," she said, after a long time.

"Still here."

"Thank you." Her voice was moist and thick, muffled by his shirt.

"For what?"

"For this. Because I know you don't understand. I know you can't feel it."

Jess took her by the chin, tilted her head until she was looking up at him. He wiped a tear from her cheek with his thumb.

"You're right," he said. "I don't understand. But who ever told you a man needs to understand a thing in order to feel it?"

She shook her head then, fresh tears pooling in her eyes, and buried her face in his shirt.

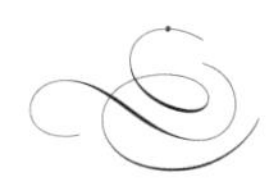

Only the day before, Jess had stacked the far wall of the back porch halfway to the ceiling with firewood. He took up three logs of scrub oak, brought them into the front room, and laid them, along with some cedar scraps from the kindling basket and a few crumpled pages of newspaper, in the fireplace. Then he struck a match on the hearthstone, touched it to the paper, and got down on his knees to blow on it, coaxing. The newspaper caught, ignited the kindling, and disappeared in a quick puff of ash. Flames licked at the logs in a fierce, hungry burst, then quieted, burning slow and steady. He found the scorch of a fire's heat on his eyeballs pleasing, tilted back on his heels, and succumbed to the fire's lure. Work could wait.

"I forget, from year to year, how friendly a fire can seem on a cold day," Gracie said.

Jess looked up, studied her face as she came into the room. Her cheeks were red-splotched, and the soft flesh beneath the curve of her lip was swollen, but she was dry-eyed. He was relieved to see it. She had brought with her a cup of tea, had her knitting basket hooked over her arm. "It tempts me to forget my work," she said. "I could put on a record. Sheherezade, maybe. Or Nat King Cole. Just sit the afternoon away."

"I can't see a thing wrong with that," Jess replied, poking the fire. "If there is a particle of dust or dirt anywhere in this house, it'll die on its own of loneliness. Hey, maybe I'll go get my *Journals* and join you. You and me and Lewis and Clark can sit before the fire together, just the four of us, like old folks, reading and knitting."

"There are other books, you know, Jess," Gracie said, but she was laughing. It was not her usual easy laugh. Not that one, like the trill of a wood thrush, which caused Jess to think hard for things to say to keep it rippling from her throat. But, a laugh nonetheless. She slid a chair close, slipped off her socks, and propped her feet on the hearth, stretching her slim, long-knuckled toes toward the fire. She fell quiet again, sipping her tea, but the silence had changed. It was no longer between them.

Jess got quiet too. He was relieved that harmony had been restored so easily and so soon, but not surprised. It was just that way with Gracie. She was as supple as a willow branch bending to the wind. With each disappointment she somehow emerged with hope intact. Her flexibility amazed him, though it was true that he marveled at it from a distance, the way a man with no legs admires a circus acrobat.

2

THE RAIN DID QUIT, just as Gracie had predicted, though not until sometime during the night. After milking, Jess ate a cold breakfast alone, because Gracie had gone early to church, then headed back to the barn for Becky. With the ground so dry before, he knew it would make for easy plowing. The big horse cast a scornful glance at the tractor parked under the shed, eyeing the machine sideways as he led her out to a spot just past the kitchen garden.

"No need to get so high and mighty," Jess chided softly, chuckling. "A half acre is all we get to turn. Gracie says a potato patch ought to be closer to the house. She's Russki, you know, so there's no use arguing."

Becky's ears flickered and twisted to catch the sound of Jess's voice. She lifted her head then, assuming a dignified air, as if to declare that work of any size was work, and not at all beneath her. She stood quiet and patient while he fastened the harness to the plow. When it was secure, he threw the reins over his shoulders and gripped the wooden handles.

"Step up, Beck," he said, and they were busting through sod, turning the last bit of yesterday's melancholy under, burying it deep under black, rich soil.

The horse plodded forward with Jess and the plow following behind. Slices of sod curved away from the blade like cloth cut from the bolt. With the sun above his right shoulder, glinting through the clouds in an uninspired way, he guided Becky in a measured path, turning her to the right or left with little more than a "gee" or "haw" at the end of each row. As she heaved through furrow after furrow, he lavished her quietly with compliments and praise.

Standing at nineteen hands, the draft horse was tall. Percherons generally topped out at seventeen. And while he allowed that her black color was acceptable, if not exactly desirable, Pat Badger claimed she was a mite leggy for the breed. But Jess didn't mind that. He was pretty leggy himself. By the age of twenty-one, he had topped out at a ropy six foot eight. She made him a good match. What the farrier deemed flaws he found endearing, only made him fonder of her. Anyway, whatever Becky might be lacking in conformation she made up for in character. Jess had never known a horse so eager to work. Sometimes, in a sentimental moment, he could almost believe she labored purely for love.

When Clyde and Millie died and it had fallen to Jess to decide how the farm should be run, he had kept Becky—a filly then, and unbroken—for the simple pleasure of training her to the harness himself. He sold the old working mare, Maggie, and her plow-mate, Big Jake. The pair had a few good years left in them and brought a fair price. It was enough for a tractor, secondhand, so Jess bought a 1938 Johnny Popper that Harlan Christie at the Feed & Seed was selling cheap. The tractor ran fine and made for quick work. Sitting high on the seat of it, though, bumping down a row with the motor growling and the exhaust popping, Jess found himself in unexpected sympathy with Clyde, for it made a poor substitute for a day in the fields with Becky, her powerful straining running through the harness reins to his hands, the smell of horse sweat, leather, soil, and grass filling his nostrils, the slap, slap jingle of tack riding the breeze.

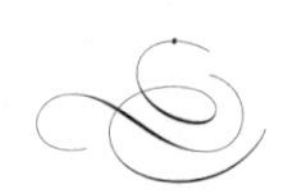

At midmorning, Gracie stood in church, waiting to make confession. A silver-haired reader had just finished chanting the hours in Old Slavonic, his voice halting and raspy, and now a younger man, long reddish-blond hair caught back in a ponytail, was beginning them all over again, this time in English. Gracie understood both. "Thou who at every season and every hour, in heaven and on earth, art worshiped and glorified, O Christ God, long-suffering, merciful, and compassionate. Who loves the just and shows mercy on the sinner . . ." He chanted in the Russian style, the words running along a straight monotone line, with one or two occasionally dipping below or above it. He was only a boy, Gracie realized, looking at him more closely, seeing the rounded flesh of his cheeks, the awkward, self-conscious way he hunched over the chanter's stand. His voice had already changed, though. It was deep and pure. No trace of an accent. That was how she intended it to be with the Hazel children. She would speak only Russian to them, and Jess would speak only English. She felt it was important that their children . . . their children . . . had it really been ten years? Who could blame Jess for doubting? But there *would* be children. And she wanted them to be at ease, as poor Jess still wasn't, with her parents. She imagined her father, grinning like an infant himself as he bounced her firstborn on his knee. It was a familiar scene, one she called to her imagination often, and it dismayed her to find the image hazy.

She turned her attention to the confession line then. It seemed longer than usual this morning. But then, autumn was the season of repentance. She'd decided that a few years ago, while standing in a line about as long as this one, eager as the rest for a chance to dust off her soul. Of course, she knew that Great Lent was the proper time for taking inventory of weaknesses and failings. And she knew too that the specially written prayers and services, especially those of Holy Week, did foster deep repentance. But her own experience and powers of observation told her that late fall—wet, cold, and barren trees and shorter days—provoked a more voluntary contrition. The autumn penitent was a melancholy spirit in search of relief.

Suddenly she found her focus, her mind peaceful again. It was for that reason that she had come: Restore unto me the joy of Thy salvation.

At last her turn arrived, and Gracie stepped forward. She kissed first the cross and the gospel and then the icon of Christ. Under the weight of his tender gaze and with Father Antony's brocade stole smelling of beeswax and incense lying heavy on her head, she laid her burden down. All the despondency she had been indulging in since discovering that she was not, this time, to be a mother, lifted away as she spoke, leaving her soul light, her mind free.

"The child of God, Galina, is absolved. In the name of the Father, the Son, and the Holy Spirit," Father Antony said, when she had finished. Gracie turned and made a small bow to those still waiting, feeling that they were each her kin. She went then and set a candle before the icon of the Holy Virgin's mother. Her request to St. Anna was the usual one, the same petition she had been making for years, but this time she did it with freshened faith. When the candle was lit and burning bright, she took a place by the door. From there she could slip quickly away after the service, and get home in time to make sure Jess ate something hot and sustaining for the midday meal.

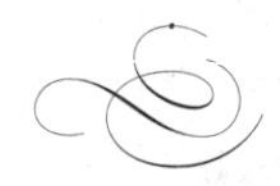

It seemed to Jess that no time at all had passed when he saw Gracie's flock of Dominicker hens come scuttling up the hill to the safety of the chicken coop. He grinned, trying to think of a sight more absurd than a chicken at a dead run. Just after the hens had gone to roost, Gracie came out of the house carrying the kitchen scrap bucket.

She stopped just inside the chicken-house door and upturned the pail, slinging in the day's vegetable peelings and the soured cheese curds she insisted on as an aid to good digestion.

He called, "Ho, Beck," and the big horse slowed, easing to a halt. Jess heard the rush of wings as the chickens unperched to see what bounty Gracie had brought.

Dusk-darkened mounds of earth now sat in rows where before there had been only sod. As he stood on the hill behind the house, gazing across the flat crest of it at the black rectangle of soil he had just exposed, his eye caught a flicker of movement east of the barn. He gathered the reins into his left hand and laid his right along his brow, squinting his eyes, filtering the haze of the evening sun. It was a person. A girl, he realized, when the tall, slight figure bent and caught her skirt in her hand, and guessed her to be about sixteen. Jess watched as the girl lifted her head, doe-like, as if to scent the air, then turned and ran swiftly north, toward the creek. He kept his eye on her until she was a speck in the distance. Then he lifted the reins and gave Becky's rump a gentle tap.

"Get up," he said.

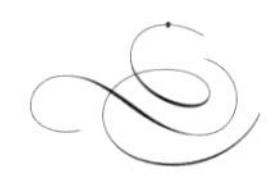

It was sundown by the time he had unhooked Becky from the plow and freed her from the harness. He stood at the edge of the turned plot with the horse at his left shoulder, squatted and picked up a clod, turned it over in his hands, then set it back down in the plot, dirt side up.

"Gracie's got some Irishers in the bin now," he said, half to himself and half to the horse. "And don't potatoes love sod. She could sow 'em, just for grins. If I dug the rows deep, any luck at all and she'd have little ones to harvest by early spring."

Becky pushed her muzzle into the small of his back. He stood and leaned against her muscled shoulder, reached up, and worked her ear with his fingers, folding it over like the finger of a glove, tugging on it absently while he considered the fruits of their labor. It was only a garden plot to be sure. A common, common thing to a farmer's wife. But the job was well done. A decent offering. All, it seemed, Jess's lot to give. Simple acts and small pleasures. Never the desires of her heart.

He turned back toward the barn, thinking that he would reward Becky with a flake or two of alfalfa and relieve his cows of their milk—creatures of such extreme habit they were already at the barn, begging to be let into the milking shed. Becky measured her step to his, kept pace with him all the way down the hill, treading on his shadow. The evening sun was no longer listless. It shone down bright and strong, touching the leaf carpet underfoot, burnishing it copper here, gold there. From the woods that bordered his fields, the odor of composting leaves and other plant matter reached Jess's nostrils on the wind. Yesterday's rain had released into the air the scent of autumn, delayed until now by a late Indian summer. Necessary as growth, the decay and dormancy stalled by drought was finally underway. The air was cool now, but he saw that the recent hot weather had fooled a migratory bird or two into lingering longer than was wise. A pair of mourning doves were among those who had missed the call. They keened softly from the barn eaves. Becky stopped to whiff an acorn lying in the path and Jess halted, waiting for her.

Gracie was brighter today, he thought, glancing up to the house where the light had gone on in the kitchen. When she returned home from church at noon, she seemed almost to have put the disappointment of yesterday behind her. But Jess knew, and only too well, that sometime, maybe not next month, or even next year, but sometime, she would have reason to believe again and they would have it all to do over.

Endometriosis. That's what Dr. Cohen at the university hospital over in Pittsburgh had written on his chart when Jess and Gracie finally consulted him after they had been married two years and still no child was on the way. He said Gracie had rogue cells growing over her womb and a baby couldn't grow inside it. Not to give up, though—she still had a 50 percent chance of conceiving. She should feel lucky to be one of those rare women for whom the condition was silent, who suffered little discomfort with it.

Jess had thought the doctor awfully glib in the delivery of his diagnosis, casually slashing their chances at a baby by half, saying Gracie didn't suffer, as if that white coat he wore were an extra layer of skin that kept him from feeling his patients' pain. But Gracie had turned to Jess with the hope of a casino gambler glazing her eyes. She seemed to think 50 percent was a sure-thing bet.

When they'd got home from the hospital and had a bite of supper, Jess eased volume nine of the *World Book Encyclopedia* set from the bookshelf in the living room and took it down to the barn with him. Once the weaning calves had drained their bottles and Becky was bedded in fresh straw, he tilted back on a sack of oats, flipped the book open under the tack room light, and read all about the witch-grass creeping over Gracie's insides. He knew then they'd been offered no sure thing.

After that, Jess had suggested adoption. He was shocked to find her reluctant. For if he had ever met a woman made to love another mother's child, it was Gracie. After a little more consideration, though, he believed he understood. Gracie was not opposed to adoption. She was opposed to accepting the fate the doctor prescribed for her. If God had pronounced her as good as barren, well then, she would have to be resigned. But a doctor was not God, so she was not resigned. Not resigned at all.

Becky nosed the acorn, rolling and sniffing the nut in an almost canine fashion. Jess watched absently. A thought struck him then, sudden and hopeful.

"Say, Beck," he murmured, "I just got myself an idea."

3

TSURA BUNCHED THE HEM OF HER SKIRT tight in her fist and ran for the creek, full breaths shoving hard against her ribs. She knew he had seen her, the man with the horse. She was sure he thought her a thief, gleaning ears of feeder corn in his fields, but time was too precious now to worry over it. The temperature was dropping fast and another rain was coming. She could feel the swell of moisture in the air, the cold and damp of the earth under her bare feet, but she would not make it home before the sun set.

Eli fretted when she didn't return before dark, but she knew there would be no scolding her this time. For days now, he had been in a spell. When his mind was turned that way, he did not mark her absence any more than he would have her presence, had she stayed to keep him company. Up on the mountain she heard the faint sound of a dog barking. Bell. The dog had followed Tsura as far as the door this morning with her tail held low and then turned back to lie down on the floor at Eli's feet. She was beginning to show with her litter, but she would have stayed, regardless. When still a pup, Bell had made it her duty to stand guard over his body—for however long his mind journeyed away.

As soon as she reached the creek bank, her feet found the hollowed path with sycamore roots stacked like the rungs of a ladder. They led her down to the spot where on opposite sides of the stream huge square stones lay in stacks almost touching and formed a kind of footbridge. She bent and grasped the hem of her skirt, pulled it through her knees, and tucked it firmly into the waistband, the way she always did when fording the stream or scaling a hillside.

She stretched her legs wide at the gap between the boulders, hungry white waters gushing beneath, and quickly crossed. Once she reached the opposite bank, she grabbed the arm of a sapling oak and pulled herself to sit on the rock it grew above, drawing a few quick, deep breaths before she began her ascent. The sun was well gone now, and she must make her way in the dark.

All the slithering creatures were bedded down for the winter. Tsura was glad for that. One hot summer night she had reached up for a root and pulled down instead a writhing pair of copperheads seeking prey together in the darkness. Too stunned to strike, the snakes fell hissing to the ledge below.

She put her hand in her pocket, shivering at the memory, and touched the little velvet drawstring pouch. Her heart wished to believe that the fresh alfalfa she filled it with each summer had some power to protect her, but it always failed just short of faith. She had too many times seen the same tender leaves being pulled up by the roots in great clumps by grazing livestock, or trampled underfoot by a deer herd seized with the urge to play at twilight. No, she carried the pouch because it had been her mother's. And filled it because Maria had thought alfalfa lucky. She opened the other pocket then and peeked in to see that the little picture she carried with her always was secure, and that the goldenrod she had gathered and dried at the end of summer was safe too, lying next to it. She had made the goldenrod into a small bouquet. She would leave it at the grave on her way up to the house.

The place wasn't marked. She touched the cross at her neck, a remnant of her mother. If Maria had known she was going to die, she might have asked Eli to make one like it, though larger of course, for her grave and he would have done it. But she hadn't known, hadn't asked, and there was no cross. There was not even a stone. Tsura had only just found her way to the spot one sunlit morning and knew it was under that hill of soft grass and Queen Anne's lace that her mother lay. Her mother. The woman, the girl, who had managed to live long enough to give Tsura her life and her name.

Her discovery of the grave had unsettled Eli.

"You could not know this. You should not know it. How is it that you know?"

Every so often, knowledge came to her with a lightning-white flash behind the sockets of her eyes. More often she was simply compelled to head in a certain direction and went, the way a bird finds her own nest in a forest thick with trees. Always she obeyed the sure, quiet, voice that urged her to each deed and action. Such doings, so natural to Tsura, Eli thought very unnatural. He did not forbid her, of course. He had never forbidden her anything. But not wishing to cause him worry, she had learned to carry them out mostly in secret.

A sudden cold breeze swirled up from the creek and she shivered, glancing around. The darkness had deepened while she sat. She rose and began to make a quick climb. Without seeing it, she knew that directly above her head the trunk of a scrub cedar sapling sprouted from a crack in the ledge. She reached up and grasped it. Then she felt around with her right foot until she located the first cleft in the gnarled limestone knee of the mountainside. She wedged her toes in tight, working them until she felt sure of their grip, then shifted her weight a little to test the strength of the rock. It held firm. Balanced on her right leg, she swung the left out and gripped with the strong, limber toes of that foot a web of exposed roots. Once she had secured her footing, she groped with her free hand for a sucker limb that protruded near the base of the hickory growing just above. In this creeping, spiderish way, she hoisted her body up the hillside, every cranny as familiar to her fingers as the folds of her own ear, until finally she breached the last set of rocks and broke out into the open.

She stopped and turned, taking a last lingering look at the valley below. The moon had risen, and in its soft white light the powerful stream she had just crossed in darkness seemed a gentle, trickling brook. In the distance, across the fields on a hilltop, the lit windows of the farmhouse shone yellow against the darker hills behind. She was not done with it, she knew. But the cord pulling her toward the valley had slackened for now.

Slowly, purposefully, she turned her back on the tall, quiet farmer and his wife, so empty-armed, and set her face toward home. Her eyes sought the crooked path to the house she had hewn and worn herself, ascending and descending Kerry Mountain. A familiar whistle reached her ears on the wind, like that of a groundhog sow calling for her young. She quickened her pace. From the back of the house just ahead, the kitchen lamps glowed. A dark figure stood silhouetted in the door. Eli was waiting.

4

HAPPEN TO KNOW where I might find a good dog?"

The farrier's grunt was the only answer Jess got to his question. Pat Badger had the lower portion of Becky's left hind between his knees and his teeth clamped around a half-dozen nails. He picked up a shoe, fitted it to the last new-trimmed hoof to be shod, pounded it into shape on his anvil, and attached it with the nails, tapping each one into the hoof wall with firm precision. Once he had checked to make sure the hoof had expansion room the width of his thick thumbnail, he let the leg drop, and Becky shifted her weight back to all four. Pat turned and gazed out the barn door for a long moment, his expression exceedingly ponderous and sober, it seemed to Jess, considering the everyday nature of the question.

"I suppose I do," he said at long last. "That is, I know where there's going to be a litter pretty soon. If you're not looking for a pure breed. The pups will be a little bit collie, but what else, I couldn't rightly say."

Though he was several inches shy of matching Jess's rangy height, turned sideways Pat made two of him, just as he once had Jess's father. And though he must be closing in on eighty about now, the man was still a mountain. Held peace like one too, conserving words as if his mouth had become permanently crimped around the tools of his trade. Jess watched him taking off his leather apron, wordlessly packing up his tools, and it struck him how important the farrier's friendship was to him. Pat's words were like his horses, tested thoroughly for soundness before he would consider sending them out into the world. It was because of this that Jess always heeded what he had to say, if sometimes he could not act as Pat advised. It had been that way when Pat encouraged him in his senior year of high school to take a scholarship he was offered to study at the state university. There was a measure of grace in everything, he said, and Jess's good mind was a gift. The scholarship, too, was a gift. So was the knowledge Jess could bring back home to share. The grace in this case, as Pat saw it, was threefold: a gift inside a gift inside a gift.

Clyde, who had never seen eye to eye with Pat Badger on much of anything (if Pat said a horse was seventeen hands, Clyde would head to the tool shed for his measuring stick), had his own view on the scholarship. Nothing, he reminded Jess, was free. "I'm not telling you not to go," his father had said, in the same gentle, persuasive tone he used to get Big Jake pulling his way, "But you can't do it thinking you'll improve yourself for this life. What they've got, well, it isn't needed here. I've seen it more than once, boys who leave these hills whole and hale and come home maimed. Either they have become profiteers, trading their birthrights for a bite of stew, or they are poets, down on their knees in the worship of nature. Misfits. All. God help 'em. In fact, I don't believe there's a creature on earth I pity more than an educated farmer."

Jess had wanted to protest, but had no example of his own to hold up, not even Pat. For with his penchant for turning workhorses into dandies, Pat was the very image of Clyde's misfit. Anyway, the truth was that be it war or education or the lure of a factory paycheck that took them away, most never returned. It was this Clyde feared. Not that Jess would come back ill-suited for farming, but that he would not come back at all. And though Jess had wished only for his father to bless him and say a plain, "Go," he would have stayed regardless, for all he'd ever wanted was to continue as he was, content. And if the peace he'd counted on was not as easy to come by as he had hoped, he had no regret over having not gone. Though he did consider, every now and again, as he was lighting a lamp, sitting down to read at the end of a long day, what things he might have learned.

Jess paid Pat in cash, insisting, as always (you had to almost pry Pat's large fist open and close the money inside), and wrote down the address of the fellow with the litter of pups. Pat had hardly pulled away when his pickup came to a halt. Jess left the barn door and strode the distance. Pat sat with great shoulders slumped, hands on his knees, blue eyes only half-visible under his wool driving cap as he gazed past Jess's shoulder at the fallow south field, his mind working at something important.

"About them pups," he said, finally. "I wouldn't be afraid to take one myself if I needed a good dog. The fellow that has 'em keeps an old buggy horse pretty long in the tooth. I've been tending to it now and again for years. He's a good customer, and a friend. But I can't vouch for him, you understand."

Jess nodded, though he didn't, of course. Didn't understand at all. He watched Pat drive away, wondering what sort of man it could be Pat couldn't vouch for, yet so readily claimed as a friend.

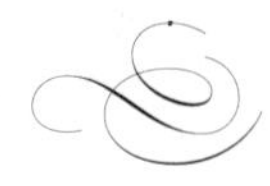

It was not long before hope showed up again in Gracie's eyes, as Jess had known it would. And seeing it, his foreboding returned.

He sensed danger ahead.

A blind fork in the road.

A frequent waking vision began to haunt him in which Gracie took her dream-child and left him at the split, the road closing up behind them so that he couldn't follow. It was distressing to have vague worries transformed into such vivid, real-seeming scenes. What he needed was to find a distraction for her, some way to shift her focus. The thought returned to get her a dog, one of those pups Pat had told him about. It was about time, after all. There hadn't been a dog on the place in years.

5

THE OLD FEED TRUCK GROANED as Jess shifted into granny gear. He ground his way up the steep, narrowly winding road, spotting, as he neared the top, a house through the bare trees—an ancient wooden frame, large and gaunt and set way back from the road, as if it disliked being seen. He pulled into the drive, just a stretch of bare packed dirt, and parked. There was another dirt path, he saw, leading from the back door of the house to a three-sided shed, freshly built, for the wood was still raw and white. Beyond it lay the wall of trees lining the cliff that jutted out over Hazel Valley. Pat had neglected to mention that these folks were Jess and Gracie's neighbors, had they been hatched out of a crow's nest.

This was the old Smiley place. The crazy old hermit woman who had lived here was already ages old when Jess was small. Violet Smiley raised pigs she coddled like children. She had been gone a long, long time, and under mysterious circumstances, as he recalled, sparking several grisly legends passed dutifully from child to child in his grade at school, the most popular one being that she had tripped and fallen one night and been eaten alive by her own hogs. That this was impossible—for Violet's whole place had been found bare of everything: hogs and chickens and rickety, threadbare old furniture, pointing more to a whisking away or a purposeful retreat than a devouring—didn't keep them from preferring it to the other stories. If Jess were a crow and flew a straight northerly path that cut through the stand of woods bordering his own east fields, crossed Muddy Creek, and continued at an angle up the sharply tilted mountainside, he would find himself at Violet's back door. His skin pricked as he dropped his long legs down from the truck and walked up on the porch, Pat Badger's cryptic statement echoing through his head. "I can't vouch for him, you understand."

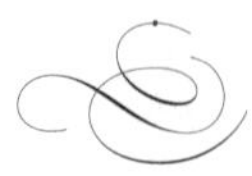

He knocked at the front door and got no answer. After waiting a moment, he went back to the truck and got the sack of kibble he had been sent to bring. He hoisted it to his shoulder, then stepped around to the back of the house, parting on the way a flock of mismatched chickens busy rolling up the leaf-rug to get at the wintering insects burrowed underneath. One Polish hen with a dramatic topknot of feathers squawked as if he meant to catch her for stew and flew up to sit on a rotting fence post.

A girl appeared like a phantom out of nowhere, skirted the corner of the house, and then vanished behind the lean-to shed.

"You got some business?"

Jess whirled. A man with a straw hat set down low over a shock of grizzled, lanky hair stood facing him. He was dressed Amish, and the accent was right, but aside from that there was not much that spoke to Jess of Plain folk. Even more out of place was the old blue Ford pickup truck Pat Badger used to drive. It was parked as if it belonged, alongside the garage.

"Got a delivery for you," Jess said, jerking his thumb toward the truck, parked with the side of the cab visible that had painted on it a rose of Sharon in full pink bloom and the words *Rose Point Feed & Seed*. Jess had been driving for Harlan Christie a couple of days a week since milk orders had begun getting whittled at the cheese factory a year ago. "Barter for an order of brooms, I was told. And I've got a bit of business of my own. Pat says you might have a litter of pups needing homes."

At that, the man turned without speaking and headed abruptly toward the shed. Jess followed behind with the sack of kibble. He hung back a little, checking around for the girl. He was sure now that it was the same girl he had seen crossing his lower field, although on that evening he had only caught a glimpse. He saw her then, on the west side of the shed, out of sight of the man. She saw that he saw and held her finger to her lips, shaking her head. As their eyes met Jess got a brief, strange sensation, almost a shock, as if he'd touched a hot electric fence. The girl broke gaze first. And Jess had the odd idea that she did it as a kind of favor, as if she knew he couldn't have managed it on his own.

The kennel the man had set up was a wonder in the rude, dirt-floored shed. A collie mix with a lustrous mane lay in a wooden whelping crate, curled around a single fat pup, working the teat. The crate was lined with fresh straw, and beside it sat two pottery bowls, a blue one filled with clean water and a yellow one with kibble. Jess dropped the sack of dog food next to the crate and folded to the ground, sitting on his boot heels to look in the box. The dog held Jess's gaze, then lowered her head to roll the satiated pup to its back, swabbing its belly with her tongue.

"Born six weeks," the man said, speaking his words hurriedly, impatiently, as if he had little time for showing pups to strangers. "She had three. Two girls and one boy. I just got this one girl left. The others was runty, only lived a few hours."

"Do you know the sire?"

The man passed his hand over his brow, settling and resettling his straw hat in the jerky, rhythmic motion of a tic. His face had a worn, tired look etched into it, the skin around his mouth permanently furrowed with lines dug deep. At the same time there was a fevered excitement about the way he spoke and moved, the look in his eye: pupils large and dark, the rim of visible iris glittering with the intense, hot blue of an August sky. When he spoke, his words were rushed, impatient.

"Yah. I know him," he said. "Big shepherd from the valley was up here during her time. He comes again, I'm gonna stick him on a pitchfork and set him out on the road for them to see that don't know how to keep a dog at home."

Jess blinked, ill at ease in earnest now. Though the care taken for the collie bitch seemed to point to its emptiness, it was a harsh statement. He couldn't help thinking of the Busco dog, the one Margit had got to guard the fruit stand when she had to leave it unattended. That dog was a huge black shepherd of some type, he knew. And a male. He went to the whelping crate and bent to let the collie scent his hand, keeping the man in full sight.

She was in obvious good health and had a peace about her Jess couldn't deny. Not the sign of an ill-handled dog. He picked up the pup. When he laid her on her back along his palm, she struggled against the position, a sure sign of wits, Clyde always said. Jess took his delivery pad out of his coat pocket and wrote on the top page.

"I'll take her." He handed first the pup to the man and then the slip, ripped from the pad. "You can call me at that number when she's full weaned."

In three long strides, he reached the truck and swung himself up by the handle. He looked around for the girl. She was at the door of the truck, holding up a small rag doll, shaking it, as if to say she wanted Jess to take it. The instant the doll was in his hand, she was suddenly gone, as if spirited away. Jess started the truck and backed down the drive, taking it slow. He saw her then, sitting on the steps of the porch. She hugged her knees and stared at Jess, her eyes boring a hole through the windshield.

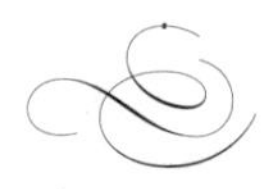

When the truck lights had gone out of sight, Eli came around the house to where Tsura was sitting on the step. He began to rave, as she had thought he would. It had been her reason for staying out of sight. She knew it would take all he had to keep a hold on his senses with a stranger about. Now that they were alone, he could let down, give himself up to the brewing storm. He was upset about the man from the valley, the "giant," he called him, and as he fretted, his words took on the sharp, rise-and-fall sound Tsura so hated to hear. Once, he stopped abruptly, paced the yard for a moment without speaking, then came back and stared at her with eyes gone wary and wild. "Why?" he shouted, as if Pat had some darker reason than dogs for sending the man to the mountain. Eli's mind was troubled for sure when it led him to mistrust Pat Badger.

Tsura barely heeded his words, all out of meaning, but she listened hard to his tone. It was rising more now and falling less. He was growing hoarse, and more and more not himself. She tried to soothe him with soft, gentle speech, with feeble reminders of Pat's friendship, knowing, even as she spoke, that she had no more power to stop the swelling roil in his head than she had to still the waters of Muddy Creek.

Yesterday, he had begun to call her Ruth.

Tomorrow he would be at the crest of this spell.

And she would be alone.

6

THE HOUSE SMELLED OF DINNER when Jess got home. Gracie was in the kitchen. She had a meat fork in her hand and tended a sizzling skillet. He could see that she was pleased, her eyes warming to the color of spiced rum, as he told her about the pup.

"A farm needs a dog," she said brightly. "Haven't I always said that? You'll see. She will be as smart as a whip. Another Gretchen."

"Sure," Jess said, wondering, as he headed out to the barn, how she could say such a thing.

Her words echoed as Jess began readying the shed for milking. Another Gretchen. Gracie had not understood, evidently, when Jess had told her the story, that there could only ever be one Gretchen. One curly haired, little yellow mutt plucked from the berm out on Highway 422, where somebody had dumped her. One foundling dog to arrive at the farm sitting on the front seat of the station wagon, Walter looking as proud as if he'd brought a girl home to meet the family. She was skinny and flea-ridden and rag-eared and had an awkward, too-long tail, but Walter loved her. Trouble was, she decided to love Clyde.

And only Clyde.

Everywhere he went from the day she arrived, Gretchen was at his heel. He'd say, "Get, dog," and she'd light out for a calf that had strayed from the herd. Or, "Sic," when a rat was bold enough to show itself in the barn, and she'd growl and bare her small sharp teeth and tear off after it. The day she died, from a blow to the head she'd irked a bull into giving her, Jess watched his father come back from burying her, his head sunk low on his shoulders, saw how his feet dragged slow as he walked across the field, having left her body beneath the rock pile. That night at dinner he hardly ate, sat so tight-lipped and downcast it frightened Jess to see him. That had lasted until the end of dinner, when Clyde looked across the table at Walter, his eyes dark and menacing, and said, "Not another goddamned stray dog, do you hear? I'll shoot it myself."

And though Walter never got the chance to bring home another dog, Jess had heard the strangle of pain in his father's voice. He had always believed Clyde meant it.

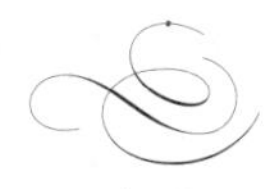

"Strange day," he said to Gracie, when they had sat down to supper. "They hired a new man to work in the warehouse. A carnie, no less. Shifty-eyed as any I've ever seen. And his name is Ace, if you can believe it. A man with a crooked eye and name like Ace drifts in the from the Butler fair, and what does Harlan do but give him a job. And then, to top that, Pat sends me up the mountain to the House of Usher, looking for a dog."

He told her then about the man, Eli Zook, his house, the feverish look in his hot blue eyes, the odd behavior of his daughter, and what in general appeared to him to be an Amish lifestyle gone weirdly awry.

"That Zook, he's strange enough. But the girl," Jess stopped, feeling hesitant, for some reason, to describe Zook's daughter. The breathtaking, dark wildness of her beauty. Her fearful gaze.

"Well, you know what they say," Gracie said, in a matter-of-fact tone, putting a thigh of fricasseed chicken on his plate along with a helping of the green beans and baby onions she had canned last summer.

"I doubt it. What do they say?"

"Where there's a door, there's a wolf."

"Who says that? Must be Russian, 'cause I don't follow." Jess reached over the stack of black rye for a slice of store-bought, the soft white stuff Gracie detested and only put out for him.

"Well, the door is a metaphor for the mind, which is the only way into the heart. And the danger is—," she broke off, shaking her head. "Forget it. Russian sayings never make sense to you. And when I try to explain, they don't make sense to me."

She was quiet for a minute, thinking. Then she said, "I haven't met Mr. Zook. But he's human, right? And don't we all suffer? We all have weaknesses. Injuries. Battle scars. Sins. Even the Amish. Straw hats and horse-drawn buggies don't buy paradise. Or else none of us would need a savior."

"Well," Jess mumbled, suddenly discomfited. He slathered an excess of butter on his bread. In a decade of marriage, he had yet to discover a better method than sidling for dealing with Gracie's religion. A pious Russian's world fairly teemed with unseen spirits, good and evil, locked in a powerful struggle over the human soul. And Jess had never known anyone who talked as naturally as they did of sin. How Gracie could be so tranquil, believing as she did, he could not fathom. Jess remembered the girl again, then, and the eerie way she had seemed to see right through—no, inside—him. He rubbed his arms, smoothing down the hairs. "There is something weird in the air up at that house. I'll give you that," he said. "Hey, I almost forgot." He stood to his feet and reached into his back pocket. He held out the rag doll. It was a little handmade thing, dressed in a dingy, white flannel gown, sewn with large crude stitches.

"How old did you say this girl was?" Gracie asked, taking the doll. She turned it slowly over in her hand to look at its face. She traced the sleeping eyes with her finger, and the tiny dash of a mouth, drawn in charcoal.

"She's one of those that makes it hard to tell. When I first saw her, I'd have said sixteen or seventeen. Now I'd guess her more at eighteen or nineteen."

"And you're sure they are father and daughter?"

"Well, I wouldn't say I was sure," Jess said. "But Zook is at least thirty years older, maybe more. One of those things you just sort of gather, I suppose."

Gracie was quiet. She held the doll in her lap, almost reverently. And on her face was a look such as Jess had seen only a few times before in their marriage, when he had interrupted her at prayer. It was a look he could never quite put there himself, however hard he tried. She sat that way for a long while, stroking the doll's head with her finger and smoothing the little dress.

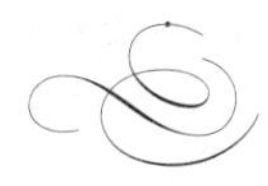

At dusk Jess stuck his head around the back door. Gracie was at the sink, washing the supper dishes.

"Got a few things to finish doing down at the barn."

"I thought we were going to look at the catalog," she said. "You need some new flannel shirts before it gets any colder."

"What's wrong with the ones I've got?"

"They're aging into Swiss cheese." She pointed with a soapy finger to a jagged hole below his shirt pocket. "That fabric's worn too thin to mend anymore."

"Maybe I should get some of those cowboy kind," he said. "The ones with the fancy piping on the pockets, and snaps."

Gracie smiled. "Maybe you should, one or two. They aren't as practical as these ones you're wearing now, though. Buttons are easier to replace than snaps. I can make the order. I just thought we were going to look at it together this evening."

"We still can. What I've got to do won't take long."

She glanced up at him, rinsing a glass.

"Wait," she said. She put the glass in the dish drainer and dried her hands on a towel.

Jess waited at the door, watching her exchange her slippers for garden clogs and her apron for a coat.

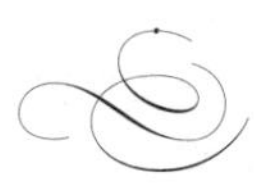

In the barn Gracie rubbed Becky's neck and let her nibble sweet feed from her palm while Jess fussed around fastening things up for the night. Unaccustomed as he was to have her with him at his work, he lingered in his tasks, savoring the moment.

It wasn't necessary, but just to stretch the time he went up to the hayloft and brought down four bales of alfalfa and stacked them in the feed room. Then he took down the tack, rearranging it on the opposite wall. After looking at it there for a while, he moved it back to its usual place. Finally, he emptied a bag of oats into the feed bin and brought out a bale of the hay, setting it against the outside wall of the tack room for Becky's morning meal. There was no more to do after that, so he walked over to the stall where Gracie stood stroking Becky's muzzle, kicking aside, as he went, an old bird's nest lying in the alley.

"What kind of nest is that?" she asked.

"Swallow, I guess. Only bird I know dumb enough to build a nursery in a barn full of cats."

"I like swallows," she said, "with their split tails and dark underwings. They look so pretty when they fly. They make me think of figure skaters, the way they slip low and fast just above the ground, then go to cutting circles way up high."

"They make an awful mess in here. That's all I know. Last year a pair of 'em raised their brood right over Becky's stall. Just a shovelful of garden dirt to mix in with all the fertilizer they made, and you might have grown a bed of spinach on her back." Jess bent and picked up the nest. It was an intricate thing, made mostly of mud pellets, lined with downy feathers and what looked to be a wad of coarse black hair stolen from Becky's tail.

"But, you are right," he said. "They are pretty. S'pose that's why I can't bring myself to run 'em off. Hey, I know a little something that'll make you like them more," Jess said suddenly. He was pleased to have a bit of knowledge he could use to impress her. "They mate for life."

"What? The same two birds come back to this barn every year?"

"That's what they say, though I can't prove it. They all look alike to me."

Gracie was quiet. She stroked Becky's nose, gazing off at something Jess couldn't see.

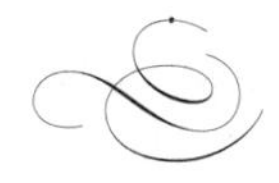

Just after dawn the next morning, when Jess had finished with the milking, he came up from below and saw the door to the hayloft was open. Climbing the stairs, he found Gracie spreading quilts across a pile of loose hay.

7

When they got into bed that night, he heard her breaths grow even almost instantly. He lay on his back next to her, elbows up, head resting in his hands. He felt wakeful, loathe to end the day. He grinned then, remembering. "Hey, Gracie," he'd said, softly, stepping through the loft door. "Hay is for horses," she'd replied. There was no milk delivered. They'd passed the entire middle span of the day up there. Just like a pair of swallows.

"What?" Gracie suddenly asked. Jess turned his head and saw that she was awake, her eyes half-open.

"What do you mean, what?"

"What were you smiling about, just now?"

"I wasn't."

"Yes, you were. Tell me."

"You were snoring like a fat old granny is all."

"Oh," she said, closing her eyes.

Jess gazed down at her. He felt as though all the goodness in all the world had flown in to roost in his chest. If he had need of a savior, as Gracie said all men did, then by God she was his.

"Jess," Gracie said, her eyes still closed.

"Hmm."

"Tell me about Walter."

"Walter?"

"Yes," she opened her eyes again. She rolled onto her side to look at him. "You know, Walter? Your only brother? The one who went to war. The one you never talk about unless it's a story from when you were boys. I want to know the man. My brother-in-law."

Jess had to admire her cleverness, for she had thought to catch him in that place between wake and sleep, when a man is least wary, vulnerable to sharing more of himself than is wise. She was right, of course. He did not talk of Walter. Tried, most days, not to even think of him. The way he saw it, brotherly love came seeded in a man at birth and grew up very naturally right along with him. Losing it was like the uprooting of a great tree. What was the use in forever standing beside a great, gaping hole, gazing into it, measuring its depth?

Suddenly every nerve he owned was on alert, the old familiar uneasiness spreading through his core, threatening to displace his peace. For comfort, he stroked Gracie's shoulder. She lay quietly, letting him work the small sharp bones with his thumb, like a child kneading the satin binding of his blanket. Her eyes burned bright in the darkness. Where there's a door, there's a wolf, she had said of the man on Kerry Mountain. What really haunted the Zook place, Jess did not know. Nor did he care. He had his own set of fangs to worry about. His was a hollow-bellied creature, forever on the prowl. Only that fire which blazed in Gracie's eyes kept it at bay.

"We'll talk about this another time, good woman," he lied then, and bent to plant a kiss on the curve of her cheek. "Just now you've got me wonderful tired."

At that, Gracie laughed gently, her voice soft and low. A sound that, for Jess, dispelled all gloom.

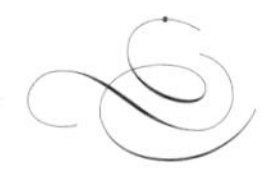

Somewhere in the darkness a rooster crowed. In her attic bedroom, Tsura woke with a start. Without rising to look, she knew that she was alone in the house. Eli was gone. Bell too. And though the knowledge pained her, she knew that this time they would not return.

There was something more she knew, for she had just seen it as she slept. The woman was no longer just one person. She was two. A child was coming to the valley below.

8

SOME WEEKS AFTER Gracie had wooed him in the barn loft, Jess woke one morning before dawn, chilled and shivering. The temperature had dropped at least ten degrees overnight, and the bite of cold was sharp. He rose from the bed, careful not to disturb Gracie, and laid an extra quilt over her sleeping form. Pausing by the bed, he stood still and quiet for a moment, fighting the urge to crawl back in next to her warmth. The moon was waning, and in the half dark her silhouette curved against the gray of the bedroom wall. His eyes traced the line that ran from her shoulder to the scoop of her waist, then made the gentle climb to the rise of her hip.

Although she dozed heavily in the early hours, she was by night a light sleeper and heard every sound, most of them common to an old, drafty house. It was hardly worth the effort, she always said, to try and wake Jess—if not calf or foal, he was dead to it, a myth he only allowed her to maintain because he was fond of watching her sit up in bed with eyes trained on the door, clutching the little gold cross at her neck for protection.

While he stood watching, she stirred, and the shape on the wall shifted, taking another, no less fetching form as she rolled to her other side. Her shadow had a new fullness to it, Jess decided, and the thought pleased him, since for years now her yearning had kept her very thin. He gazed a second longer before turning reluctantly away, heading for the kitchen and a cup of coffee.

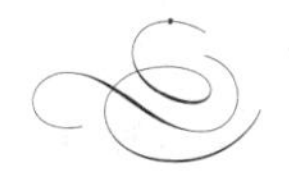

Once the percolator had done its job and he had finished off a first steaming cup (filling-station coffee, Gracie always called it, disdaining to partake), he began to hunt around for something to read. He spied an envelope then, perched atop yesterday's newspaper. It was addressed to him but unsealed. Gracie had already opened it. When Jess looked at the date, he saw why she had. It was the letter Pop had delivered in the rain, weeks back. She must have found it in the pocket of his coat. He shook out the contents. There was a note, handwritten on plain blue stationery and sent in an airmail envelope, which was addressed to Clyde and Millie at the farm. Folded inside the note was a photo. Half a photo, rather. It had been torn down the center, separating a couple. The picture had been taken from a distance, but it seemed to Jess that the girl in it was happy. She smiled, anyway, squinting into the sun, one hand reaching for a dark curl that had escaped her scarf, the other tucked into the pocket of her coat. A set of square-nailed male fingers curved around her waist. Jess unfolded the letter.

Dear Mr. and Mrs. Hazel,

I'm real sorry it's taken me so long to write this. My wife says I'm a man of good intentions and that's mostly all. Awful sorry, too, about your son. All these years, and I still feel bad that I got to come home, and he didn't. Walter was a good friend of mine, good friend to all the guys in our company, always trying to keep our spirits light, which wasn't as easy as it sounds. I know I could get real low sometimes, especially at night. It was awful cold and dark as a cave in our bunkers at night. If I would light one of the candles my mother sent regular, so I wouldn't have a reason not to write, Walter would tell us about your farm. The way he described it sure could take your mind off things for a while. I used to ask him if he was sure he wasn't Jewish, the way he talked on all the time about the promised land. To a boy from Detroit, it seemed like a stretched tale, all those woods thick with deer and wild turkey, the cold rushing creeks and the green of your wide, high-rolling hills, all that milk and honey, but I did always want to visit someday and see for myself. Maybe I still will. I hope to stay here on earth awhile longer, and the doc says there's no reason why I shouldn't, so long as the one kidney holds out. But I know for sure that when I do leave this world, I'm going to a bleaker, colder, darker hole than any old bunker in Korea ever was. I'm not a righteous man, and that's just the plain truth. The only mercy I can wish for is that my side of the river will be in ear's reach of Walter's, so's we can pick up the stories where we left off.

I was wounded on patrol the night before we were set to move on Pork Chop Hill. Took my bullet in the lower back where it nicked a kidney, which is why I've only got the one. Knowing I'd be going home, and he might not, Walter gave me this photo. Asked me to make sure she stayed safe, as if he was handing me a real girl and not a picture of one. I've kept it all these years. I suppose because it reminded me of something I wanted to make sure and not forget. You see, Walter never carried any of us across a river on his back or did anything else Washington would call an act of honor, as far as I know. But there ought to be a medal. For lightening a brother's load. For keeping his feet from sinking. For shining just enough light for him to see by. My God, how he could make us laugh. The candle stub is from the last night he told stories in our bunker. I stuck it behind my ear when I left for patrol. It was still there when I was carried into the hospital in Japan. I guess I hope maybe you'll light it in his memory. And think of me too.

Sincerely yours,

Howard Koch

Jess gazed at the photo, seeing a thing he had not wished to, even from the safety of Gracie's arms, as it rose unbidden to the light for a reckoning.

Walter, the evening before his departure, coming into the milking shed to undress his heart and lay it bare to Clyde. And Jess, eavesdropping from the milk room, listening spellbound as his brother confessed a deep and abiding love for a girl named Maria. Jess felt again the shock, the quick stab of pain he had felt then, as he realized Walter had kept him in the dark. More painful for Jess was the reminder that in the life of brothers there inevitably comes that closing of a door that has always stood open, the end of innocence and all the freedom of boyhood, a time that for Jess and Walter had begun according to nature but could not end in the same way. What should have been a brief period of secrecy and separation now stretched into eternity.

9

WALTER WAS SMITTEN. He wanted to marry the girl. This Jess heard him say one evening during milking. Jess had known something was on Walter's mind, for he usually rushed through Friday-evening chores, eager as he always was to get to town. That night he had gone about his work in quiet, moving around the barn at a slow, thoughtful pace. Then, midway through the milking, he had risen suddenly from his stool. Taking the partially filled milk bucket with him, he left the cow waiting and approached Clyde at his own. When Walter was finished speaking, Clyde milked in silence for what seemed to Jess an eternity. When he spoke at last, without raising his head from his task, it was in a voice so cold and jeering Jess knew without seeing them that his father's gray eyes were as flat as stones.

"What you are pining for, Walter," he said, "is known among men as a gypsy slut. It's an old tale, to be sure. Don't be the fool who tells it."

And that was the end of the matter. Almost.

The girl herself had come to the farm once, after Walter had gone. The katydids had been harping about the heat, Jess remembered, so it must have been well into summer. They had all been sitting down to dinner when the bell rang. Millie had got up to answer, calling, once she was there, for Clyde. She had come back to the table alone, saying Clyde was going to drive the girl back to the gypsy camp in the truck. Dinner was well over—dishes all washed and dried and put away in the cupboard—when he returned. It was Jess's guess that she had been given more than a lift home, for she had never come around again.

Now, Jess gazed again at the photo. He ran his finger along its torn edge. He touched the dimple in the girl's cheek, brushed with his thumb the fingers of his brother's hand. So, Clyde had not managed to level Walter's hope after all. Hadn't turned yearning into old, tired lust. Here was the proof. Carried in a pocket, perhaps, next to Walter's heart as a talisman against Clyde's anti-blessing. There seemed something almost holy about the photo, then, like one of Gracie's icons.

Jess slipped it into his shirt pocket. The image of his carefree brother's courage. Material evidence, Gracie would say, of an unseen reality.

10

LATER THAT MORNING, when Jess had turned the cows out on hay, he drove over to the Hays place. The pump on the well had a faulty switch, and he wanted to see what needed to be done to fix it. Gracie's parents, Ivan and Darya, were coming to visit. And if Jess knew anything, it was that it would not do to have Morozovs in the house and no water for tea.

More than a decade of marriage to Gracie, and he still couldn't warm to his in-laws.

Nor, he knew, could they warm to him.

Gracie was their only child, born when Darya was forty-seven, and Jess had stolen her away. It was from her mother that Gracie had got her suppleness, her strong, lithe limbs. They walked about the earth as water would, if it had arms and legs. Only in the last few years had Darya finally started showing her age, growing heavier and slower now with every year that passed. She had Gracie's amber eyes too, but Darya's were cooler and flickered with impatience at Jess's bashful fumbling. Once in a while he thought he caught the scantest, palest flash of her daughter's kindness in them, but it came and went so quickly he could never be quite sure.

Gracie's papa was a man of medium height, or slightly more (the top of Ivan's head would reach Jess's shoulder, anyway, if they were to stand side by side), with a thick, wide chest and strong old miner's arms he seemed always to keep crossed. He was balding, and what hair remained stood in two funny, owlish tufts atop his head. Gracie and her mama were joined at the heart, but it had always been Ivan who hung the moon over Gracie's earth at night. There were times when, with no small amount of jealousy, Jess suspected she also gave her father credit for the sun. On occasions like this evening's dinner, with Ivan and Darya and Gracie all together at once, Jess was the fourth leg on a three-legged stool. An awkward leg he made too, cut of inferior American wood, far too long and poorly turned. He set the whole stool off its neat little feet.

He had reached the Hays place, a piece of wooly, untilled land Orville and Zodie had bought tamed and let go wild. Zodie was a dowser, a water-witcher. With a forked stick, she found water, and with a special rig and truck, Orville brought it up. The witching was something Jess's family had never taken seriously, though it was a fact that the Hays had a high rate of success at striking water on the first try. Gracie was never skeptical when there was the scantest reason to believe, though, and would have Zodie and her wand at the farm in an instant, Jess knew, if the Hazel well should ever run dry.

"What's the news, Jesse?" Orville said. "Don't never see you this time of the day, 'less it's in the feed truck."

"Well trouble," Jess said. "Bad switch or some odd thing. Leaves us bone dry at times. Where are you going with your wife's good laying hens, Orville? Those aren't fryers, so I know you're not taking them to the sale."

"I guess you didn't hear," Orville said, leaning against the hood of the truck. "As of last week, I ain't in the well business no more. Hasn't been too enjoyable of late, anyhow, what with young folks rushing off the farms like rats in a flood."

"I'm not going anywhere," Jess said, taken aback.

"You ain't," Orville said. "But you ain't like the rest, Jesse boy. And your well don't need more'n a look-see, maybe once a blue moon. You can't keep me in a living thataway. No more'n Pat Badger can survive shoeing that one draft horse you keep just for fun. Him and me will be down to the welfare office together, holding hands." Orville grinned. He paused to pull out his tobacco pouch, pinched a generous wad between his fingers, and filled his lean cheek. After working the tobacco soberly for a while with his tongue, he spat on the ground in a thick brown stream. "I won't be one of those who goes on all the time about the good old days. They wasn't good for all, and that's a fact. But it did used to be that the first thing a pair needed after a honeymoon was a parcel of family land and a tap of good water from deep underground." He wiped his mouth with the back of his hand, his hand on the hip of his pants. "Them were good days for me. And they're gone. Young folks now have got some need to live right up agin' one another and drink that bleachy town water from plastic pipes."

Jess shook his head. "Not me. I hate town water."

"I done told you, Jesse. We ain't figurin' you into this. All I know is what used to be ain't no more. And Zodie says if we must be poor again, she wants to do it in the company of our own. So that's what we're doing. Headin' home. Truth? After forty years I still can't think of these hills as mountains, anyhow." Orville grinned, then spit. "Guess I'd just a whole lot rather be up in mama's lap than messin' about her feet." He put his truck in gear. "Now, I'd come and rewire your switch or whatever needs doing, just for old time's sake, Jesse boy. You know I would. But these hens ain't gettin' any younger. I'd better get 'em to the sale." His expression changed then, into a look Jess would never have believed had been on the face of Orville Hays if he hadn't seen it with his own eyes. It was, as Jess later described it to Gracie, downright tender, almost motherly. He stared in shock as Orville, whose eyes had grown moist, took out a grimy handkerchief and wiped them.

"Zodie says I'm gettin' as weepy and as windy as an old preacher man," he said, wadding the handkerchief into a ball, closing his fist around it. "And I can't argue with her. I tell you, Jesse, leavin' this valley has me feelin' kindly toward folks in some way I didn't used to. Get to thinkin' up all sorts of loving things to say to 'em before I go. Before we ain't neighbors no more." He shook his head. "It's pathetic."

"I could use a word, Orville." Jess said seriously.

"I ain't got much," Orville said, looking bashful now, and unmistakably pleased. "But, I guess I have been thinkin' on you some. Thinkin' of your pap, and how all-fired stiff-necked he could be. Now, I know I ain't tellin' you nothin' in that. But there's a way seems right to such a man. Oft times it isn't. Just flat out isn't. I guess what I'd say to you is it's all right to seek a map. Ask for help. There ain't a bit of shame in getting yourself pointed in the right direction."

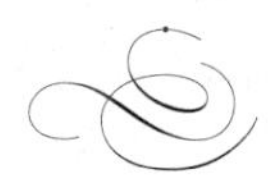

Jess had always had a great deal of respect for folks like Orville and Zodie Hays. If you could part the thorns and brambles, weren't so thin-skinned you couldn't take the scratches and pricks, you could learn a great deal from their speech. He understood, thinking it over as he was driving home, that Orville was leaving a scrap of himself in his words, much as the old will seed their neighbor's homes as death draws nigh—bringing them the seeds of a strain of pepper hot enough to swell their lips and bring tears to their eyes, or the chair they always sit in when they've stopped by on their way to town—things that have no value other than the power to keep calling the person to mind when they have been long gone.

And this word Orville had left him—seek a map, ask directions—it was good seed. Jess wasn't saying it wasn't. It was having Orville bring Clyde into things that had him pondering again as he followed a meandering Muddy Creek road past snug, smoking houses and snow-draped fields, taking the long way around Kerry Mountain to get home.

His thoughts were not easy ones.

Those nights so long ago when he had lain awake listening to the folks argue.

He heard again the sound of his mother's gentle weeping. Only now, just before she broke down in tears, Millie's tone was not one of disagreement. She was pleading.

"There's no other way, Clyde. Only this one is right."

"My dear Millie, there is never only one way to do a thing. No one right, nor ever one wrong."

They were at some crossroads. His father wanted to go in a direction his mother didn't like. A way that was terrible wrong to Millie.

Knowledge seeped slowly into Jess's bones, like the ache of an oncoming illness. He knew it was all true, and at the same time that it couldn't possibly be. He saw his mother, pictured her deliberately, seated on a stool in the barn, her spare, slight frame wrapped in his father's big canvas coat, shoulders hunched against the cold, reading paperback westerns to Clyde as he milked. And there were his parents at the kitchen table, their dark heads (they had only a strand or two of gray between them) set close together, poring through seed manuals or going over accounts in the farm's ledgers. In the light of such companionable images, his disquiet should have eased obediently away, but there was the photo of the girl, burning like a hot coal of truth, in his shirt pocket.

He happened to know a thing about gypsies that went crosswise with what Clyde had said that evening to Walter, for he had once seen a gypsy man slap his daughter silly outside the door of Latona's Deli, just for flirting with Mike. And the truth of it was that the girl had not been flirting at all. She'd only flinched away when Mike tried to grab her by a handful of skirt. To her father just coming out the door, it must have appeared like a flounce designed to fetch, for the man hit her hard, causing her to stumble and fall, knocking her head against the heavy glass window. Jess's gut had twisted as she righted herself and straightened her dress, only to have her father take her by a coil of her dark hair and drag her away. She never made a sound. Mike had laughed, though, an obnoxious "heh, heh, heh," telling his brother Sully about it inside the deli.

Sully had laughed too. "Heh, heh, heh."

Things had changed a great deal since that incident. Gypsies were either far fewer now, or they were far harder to pick out of a crowd. And it was unlikely that a father of any sort would feel free to slap his child about the head. Not in public. There were no laws against that nasty laugh of Mike's yet, though. And that was too bad. That laugh still gave Jess a pain in his gut.

Before the photo, Jess hadn't thought to consider whether Maria might have had a father like that girl's. But what if she did? If she'd had trouble because of Walter, it could have brought her to the house that night looking for him. And if it did, then this was the cause of Millie's tears. It would also be why the arguing had finally halted, for she might plead with Clyde, even push, but she would never cross him. Like Jess, she feared worse than a disease the awful weight of his silence.

But even as he acknowledged, with a kind of vague dread, that one thing might have to do with the other he saw his father's face, set hard as cast iron. *Don't neb in another man's mess, Jesse. You'll be the one with shit on your nose.* And taking the photo from his pocket, he slid it into the glove compartment and slammed the door shut. The clang of metal against metal rang through the cab. The sound was both hollow and filled with shame. Jess ignored it, wiping the sweat from his hand on the knee of his pants. He jerked down the window and put his head out, feeling the sting of cold air on his face.

When he reached home, he swung the truck around at the drive and pulled down to the barn. Gracie was sharp-eyed when it came to spotting trouble, and she knew about the letter. He needed to gather his wits entirely before going up to the house. Something was amiss, though—he could tell that as soon as he stepped through the door. Becky was all kinds of nervous, tossing her head and rolling her eyes. “Ho, Beck,” Jess said softly, looking quickly around. And there, crouched on a hay bale in the corner, was the girl, huddled under a ratted old sleigh blanket with a dog. She clutched the dog to her chest, staring at Jess with black moon eyes.

11

While Jess was bringing his mind around to accept what his eyes already knew—that the girl with the wise look he'd tried hard to forget had slipped down from the mountain and was sitting before him on a bale of last year's hay—Gracie stood in the kitchen up at the house with her back to the warm stove, waiting for the buzz of the kitchen timer.

She was baking prosphora, loaves of communion bread, for church. The yeasty smell had gone from the kitchen, and she knew the bread would soon be done. The timer went off then, and she turned to the oven and took out the loaves. There were five of them, small and round. She set them side by side on a wire rack to cool. With a finger, she soberly traced the letters imprinted in the center of each one. ICXC. Jesus Christ. NIKA. Conqueror of hell and death. The action was a prayer, a love letter. The bread she had formed with her hands, pressed in the old way with a carved wooden seal and then baked to a tender brown crust, would become in a mystery the very body of Christ that she herself would then be given, as medicine from a spoon, to eat in Holy Communion. She did not take the task lightly, and never contemplated it too long. She covered the loaves with a cloth and left them on the counter to cool.

Going to the sink where the breakfast dishes were soaking, she picked up a brush and began absently scrubbing the stains from a coffee mug. She had another mystery now to contemplate: the secret quickening of life in her womb.

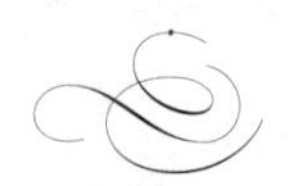

Jess and the girl climbed the hill in silence. From the corner of his eye, he saw her staring at the big stone house as they climbed, and he wondered how the structure, so dear to him, appeared to her eyes. In winter, unadorned by foliage, the house stood tall and square and starkly plain. But inviting, too, he thought, with its wide-hipped front porch and two smoking chimneys, especially when you compared it to Zook's bleak place. It was plain, though, for aside from a quilt of fieldstones, harvested during clearing and cobbled to the outer walls, it had not been built to delight, only to endure.

The quiet was broken suddenly by the loud honking of geese. Somehow Jess had missed the low approach of the flock. The girl had not. She stood as still as a post, the dog held tight to her chest, gazing up at the sky. The birds were straight above the house now, so close you could hear each one's separate cry, the beat of its wings. The geese were not keeping to a V pattern as they flew but cut a straight line below the clouds. There was a fair space of sky between the flock and the lead goose. She had taken a premature notion to head home, it seemed, and the others were scrambling to follow. In a matter of seconds, the whole long line was gone, just a faint dark spot on the quiet blue sky. When Jess looked over at the girl, the hair stood up on his neck, exactly as it had that evening on the mountain, when she'd stared him down from Zook's porch step.

There was no curiosity in her expression. No awe.

She had a look of alarm, as if the geese had been a flock of ghosts.

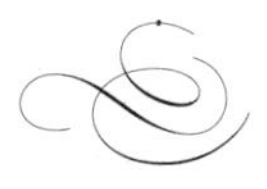

At dinner that evening, Jess was in a foul mood, sullen because the Morozovs had come, and because Gracie had laid the drop-leaf maple table in the dining room, the one room in the house she and Jess never used. They always ate in what Jess felt was good, plain comfort at the knotted, wide-planked table his grandfather had fashioned when the big oak at the corner of the lane was struck by lightning. Jess disliked the dining room. He thought it a foolish waste of space. It was small and cramped, filled with fussy furniture and crystal glass and delicate bone china, objects he could never reconcile with what he knew of Hazel women.

And there was fish for dinner.

Margit Busco's grandsons, Lester and David, were well grown boys now, men if you believed the draft board. The younger one, David, had been to the creek that morning and snagged a huge brown trout he had then brought to Gracie. To please her father, Gracie had made it the main course. This rankled, for Gracie knew (and he knew that she knew) how much Jess hated fish. In preparation for pretending to be all right with it, he drank two glasses of whiskey before dinner.

During the meal, Darya and Gracie sat with their chairs pulled close together, talking in Russian. Ivan sat next to the girl, keeping her plate ("No fish? You are sure? Well, have some more potatoes then.") and his own filled. The girl ate hungrily, but quietly—unaware, or unconcerned, that she was the subject of their talk. Gracie's hands were flying the way they only did when she was excited. Seeing her so animated made Jess jealous, glum to be reminded that he was not the only one who could add such a spark to her eye. Put by the whiskey in a mood to quietly sulk, he reached across the table for the wine and filled his glass to the rim. In a single long swallow, he drained it. Their voices floated up to his ear a good deal easier now, as if from a fog-draped lake. It would take another glass or two, though, to be fully soothed. He shoved his plate aside and reached for the bottle—a clumsy jerk of his arm that knocked his wine glass against the bottle. There was the clank and tinkle of glass against glass followed by a thud, as the bottle fell with a clatter against the table, and then silence. The sudden hushing of Morozovs.

Instantly there followed a bustle of activity. Darya began to rearrange her napkin in her lap, and Ivan reached quickly for the fish platter, sticking his fork into the trout's staring head. In a single motion he slid it onto his plate and fell to eating. He nodded to the girl, who had gone very still, winked his right eye, and made a motion with his fork to show her that it was all right for her to eat.

Jess was not soothed now. He was surly. He turned to Gracie, casting her a dark look.

"Well?"

She shot back a dark look of her own.

"Well what?"

"Well, what have you all decided?"

"Decided?" Her eyes flashed yellow. A warning.

Bolstered by the wine, Jess ignored it.

"Yes, decided," Jess said, drawing his words out, so she wouldn't miss the sarcasm. "You've been at it all evening. Looking her up and down, talking her over like three old cabbage-eaters haggling at a county fair. I don't know if you've noticed, but she's a girl, not a goat."

Gracie's lips pinched. She went pale. She laid her napkin across her plate and pushed her chair back.

"What on earth is wrong with you, Jess? Are you drunk?"

"No," Jess said, after thinking it over. The whiskey had been before dinner. A single glass of wine. He was not exactly sober, but hardly drunk. "Why?"

"Because you'd better hope you are. Because if you can say such things sober . . ."

Jess stared at her in wonder, the fog clearing from his head. It was a strange, strange thing to draw such ire from Gracie. There was a tinge of concern in her voice too, below the anger, and he was suddenly sorry he had put it there. But before he could begin in any kind of earnest to undo what was done, the dog rose from the floor and groaned anxiously, a long, low whine.

"Hush," someone said, and a half second later Tsura's eyes rolled back in her skull, showing the whites. She was on the floor then, her long, thin body limp.

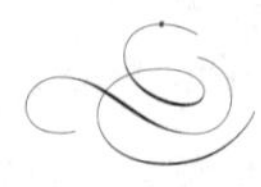

Doc Bloom came, the grizzled, ill-tempered old doctor who had delivered both Walter and Jess at home. And who, because he liked to drive his old bat-winged Cadillac deadly fast through the hills and curves, still made emergency house calls.

Doc felt Tsura's pulse and took her blood pressure, listened soberly to her heart and lungs, and shined a light into each of her wide, dark eyes, speaking to her in a gentler, more grandfatherly tone than it was his custom to use, the one he saved for delicate old ladies and very ill children. Then, when he had finished and was folding his stethoscope into his bag, he turned to Gracie and said, "She's anemic. I've taken blood to test the levels. But that's just for my files. Nothing serious, anyway. I can see that looking at her. She's just a mite undernourished. You feed her on beef liver and turnip greens, and she'll be feeling stronger in no time. Some of that good Hazel Valley milk wouldn't hurt either, to flesh out her bones. Full fat, all the cream and butter she wants."

Jess walked Doc out to his car, and opened the door for him. The old man slid in and worked his paunch behind the wheel, cussing a blue streak the whole time. "Better ask Gracie to come in and see me at my office tomorrow, Jesse," he said, finally reaching for the key, still in the ignition. "I've a pretty good hunch she's expecting."

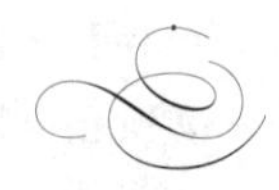

Next morning Jess drove Gracie into town, to see Doc Bloom at his office. After the examination, when they had got back in the car to drive home, Jess turned sideways a little in his seat to look at Gracie. The only words she had spoken to him since the night before had been short and cool. And she hadn't said anything since Doc had confirmed his suspicions and given them the news.

"You still mad at me?"

Gracie didn't answer. She only blessed herself, drawing a long, slow cross.

"No, I'm not mad," she said at last. Her eyes were soft gold, filled with awe. "You know, Jess, I've wondered for a little while—and then yesterday, a wispy little fluttering, like the hatching of a moth."

She went on: "And I wanted to tell you last night, but you were so—Jess, did you hear it? A heart no bigger than a raindrop, Doc said—but what a sound! I don't think I'll ever be angry again. At you, or anyone else. It would be blasphemy."

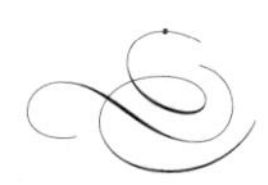

In the glow of her own happiness, Gracie asked Tsura to stay at the farm, and seemed as pleased to have her as if she were family, a beloved sister or cousin. Jess, on the other hand, was not pleased at all. He could not claim she was any trouble, of course. No more than a stray cat or dog would be, anyway. And since he couldn't explain, could in no way say to Gracie, "It's the eyes. I can't take 'em," he stayed a safe distance from Tsura, and kept his uneasiness to himself.

12

"We have nuns," Gracie said, at lunch one Sunday afternoon, hanging up the kitchen phone. She turned away from the wall and looked at Jess, her face alight. She glowed these days, since learning of her pregnancy, but there was something other than that happiness in her expression now. It was a look Jess couldn't define, other than to think it was part soberness, part joy.

"Nuns," he repeated, feeling that he should say something. She had spoken with such an air of importance, as if she'd been the first to tell him something he had been dying to hear.

"Yes, nuns," she said, with an impatient little nod. "They've bought Orville and Zodie's place at Mill Bend. The abbess is from the Romanian nobility. Maybe even the royal family. That's what Mama heard. Anyway, they were all exiled. The chaplain was in the camps, Mama said. He's suffered."

"How nice," Jess said drily, unable to help the sarcasm, for he saw how Gracie's eyes shined as she talked of the poor priest who was likely to have been tortured, had surely been beaten, starved. Lord, how Russians loved suffering! Why nuns were such a celebration was only more for Jess to try and fathom. Of course, the only nun he had ever known was the teacher Mike had for seventh grade at Sacred Heart School. Sister Vittoria was a tall, straight-faced woman with upright posture and a purposeful stride, who walked about town both summer and winter wearing thick, black stockings and sturdy, crepe-soled shoes. Creep-soul, Mike called the shoes, insisting that was her whole purpose for wearing them. Jess had never actually met Sister

Vittoria, though Mike had pointed her out to him once at the deli, but he knew none of the Latona kids cared for her. So, while Gracie was clearly thrilled to have nuns about, he did not think he should be blamed too much for failing to share her joy.

Gracie soon began to go out to Mill Bend and visit the monastery regularly, taking Tsura with her, the two of them bearing gifts of fresh milk and cream and a bounty of corn and tomatoes and cucumbers from the garden. Jess could hardly protest, for there was plenty. And Gracie glowed for days after those visits with a peace he could bask in.

13

TSURA STOOD IN THE CREEK one afternoon, cold water swirling around her bare knees. She had just spied a crayfish. She reached down, and pinching it gently between her fingers, lifted it up to her face so she could look it in its funny eye. The crayfish whipped its tail back and forth, flicking her skin with long whiskers. Suddenly a voice called from the bank.

"Looks like we had the same idea."

It was Jess and Gracie's neighbor David Busco. She had seen him coming through the woods as she crossed the field. As plain as if she had asked him to join her, he sat down and took off his shoes, tossing them over his shoulder, where they landed somewhere in the grass, out of sight. When the shoes were gone, he bent over and began to roll up the legs of his blue jeans. Tsura lowered the crayfish to the stream, opening her grasp. It made for the nearest rock and vanished in a puff-cloud of silt. The boy had crept barefoot along the bank until he had found a good, wide place. Now he was leaping into the air like an old bullfrog, landing on his feet in the stream.

"Yikes!" he yelled. "Lots colder than I remembered. Are you used to it yet?"

Tsura didn't answer. She curled her toes, pushing them deeper into the mud. He was fording the stream now, passing through the deep pool in the middle, getting wet up to his waist, paddling the eddies with his big flat hands. Up onto the bar he went, down into the shallows. Careful as a buck deer, he picked his way across the rocks, came right over to where she stood. So close she could smell him.

Her sense of smell was keen. She always knew by the scent left behind when a raccoon had been sifting the garbage pile or a possum had stopped by the chicken yard. Eli had smelled of lye soap. Unless he was in one of his spells, then he grew rank. And though it had been fainter as the years passed, the brown silk dress she used to take out from the trunk now and then, to feel its softness like a caress, had never stopped smelling of lilacs. She had often held it to her nose, inhaling sweet memories not her own. Exhaling the darker ones that tried to linger. This boy's pungent odor confused her nostrils. It was sharp, but good, too, like pine sap. She stared at the water.

"You just never shut up, do you?" he said, looking closely at her.

His eyes were friendly and eager, bright blue stars against his tanned, freckled skin. Suddenly he winked. She realized then that he'd been teasing her, and she smiled. He moved closer. Tsura stayed very still. The cold mud sucked at her feet and made them ache. But she hated to pull them out. His shoulder was almost touching hers, he stood so near.

"Ever fish this crick before?"

"Yah. Lots of times."

"I've got string and hooks in my pocket and a jar of worms over under that tree. We could wet a line."

Tsura relaxed. "Too late for that, I think," she said, pointing to his soaked blue jeans.

David worked his hand into the wet pocket of his pants and brought out a soggy knot of string. He squeezed the water from it, flashing her a wide, sheepish grin. "What I meant was, do you want to go down there where it's deeper? Sit on the root of that big sycamore and see what bites? I've got a fair-sized trout out of that pool more than once."

"Yah, okay."

He reached out and took her by the hand, as naturally as if they were old friends and not a boy and girl who until now had been acquainted only by waves of their hands from a distance. He kept her easily balanced as they walked, making their way over to the tree roots that jutted out from the bald creek bank.

"'Course," he said, "we'd do better with bread-balls, or corn, if we wanted to catch trout. Bluegill ain't bad eating, though. You just need a pretty big mess of 'em to make a meal."

"Oh, yah. Bluegills is good eating. For sure," Tsura agreed, though she did not eat fish herself. It was Pat Badger who said bluegill—sunfish, he called them—made a plenty good dinner if you fried 'em up crisp in a pan. He would have liked her to do that, she knew, fry some fish up in a pan, instead of grazing on what she could gather in her hands as she walked through the woods and fields. But she had lived a pretty long time, eighteen years, without making a meal of anything she had ever, even once, looked in the eye.

When they had reached the spreading roots of the big sycamore, he kept hold of her hand until she climbed up and sat down. Once she was seated, wringing the water from her skirt, he swung himself up beside her. He unwound the ball, patiently untangling the strings from the hooks. Steam rose from their wet clothing in the heat. Tsura was silent, gazing at her feet. Her toenails were black with creek mud.

He began tying the first line, forehead knotted in concentration. When the hooks were tied, he reached into a canvas bag at the base of the tree and pulled out a half-pint jelly jar full of dirt and fat night crawlers. He lifted a smallish one from the jar and deftly wadded it around the hook. Tsura looked away. It was only a worm, but she did not wish to see it impaled on a hook.

"How old are you?" he asked, covering the worm with his hand, as if he had understood that it bothered her to see it squirm and writhe.

"Eighteen."

"You look older," he said. And then, "I'm going away soon."

"Yah, I know. I heard Gracie and Jess talking something about it."

"Oh, yeah? What did they say?"

"Just that you will go to the war."

"I've been drafted. That's when you don't have a choice. You just get to go for a soldier."

"Yah. I know."

"You know everything. Do you like a switch, or do you just want to dangle the line from your fingers?"

"I don't care. Both is different from the way I fish, usually."

"How do you fish, usually?"

"Like this," Tsura said, grinning. She pretended to net a fish with her hands.

Still holding the line, he looked at her sharply, skeptically, then admiringly. "Well," he said, handing her the string, "maybe you can teach me how to do it your way some other time. That seems like work, and I'm feeling awfully relaxed right now. Believe I'd like a switch."

He took out a slim pocket knife and opened it. From down near the feet of the tree, he cut a slender branch. Using the knife, he made a small green wound near the end, and then fitting the string, with baited hook dangling, into the slot, he tied a knot to hold it in place. He handed the makeshift rod over to Tsura, then repeated the process with his own line, dropping it into the water and leaning back against the sycamore's wide trunk.

Tsura scooted back in the same way he had done, until she rested next to him. She bobbed her pole a little to check the tension in her line and found it was slack. She stole a sideways glance at him. He was looking at her through half-closed eyes.

"That's some hair you got," he said dreamily. "The exact color of ripe mulberries."

"My father was a soldier," she said, to deflect the remark. She felt the sting of blood in her cheeks and did not wish him to know how much it had pleased her.

"I thought the Amish were against war," he said. "That's what my grandmother says, anyway. But she doesn't care much for the Amish.

Claims they've got everybody swindled with their quaint old ways." He grinned, closing his eyes. "I've got a hunch she's really only sore at one or two. Those that have cut in on her fruit-stand business."

Tsura turned to gaze at him. His eyelashes were long, white, and spiky and made her think of dandelion seeds. "Amish are against war," she said. "But Eli is not my father. He is not Amish, neither. Not for a long time."

"Either."

"What?"

"You said Eli was not Amish, neither. You should say either."

"Either," Tsura said obediently.

He sat up then and looked directly at her, curiosity sparking in his eyes.

"Well, that explains a lot. You talk Amish, but you sure don't act it. Or look it—neither," he grinned. "How come you lived up in that creepy house with Zook, if he wasn't your old man?"

"My old man?"

"Your father."

"Oh."

Tsura jerked her line and sat up, peering soberly into the pool. She tried to look surprised to see that the worm still dangled from the hook.

"You got a bite?"

"Nah," she said, slyly, leaning back. "Just a little minnow, chipping at the worm."

"Oh. Well, there's lots more worms in that jar, if you need to rebait."

Just as she had designed, he forgot his earlier question. He leaned back again, closing his eyes.

"You ever been out to McConnell's Mill?" he asked lazily. "Seen the gorge? Or the falls at Hell's Hollow?"

"I never been nowhere," Tsura said. "Just here. Eli went sometimes to town, in the truck. But he don't take me."

David peeled back one eyelid and observed her for a long moment, then closed it again without speaking. Tsura went back to tending her line.

Eli. Some days her heart felt so heavy she could hardly lift her feet to walk. She missed him that much. Other times she remembered his bad spells and her bones felt bird-hollow.

Last night she had seen him in a dream. He lay on his back in a field of red-eared wheat. All around the field were his people, cutting the wheat by hand, and there was Eli in their midst, fast asleep. Though they seemed not to be careful of him—the men swung their sharp-bladed scythes in great sweeping arcs, sometimes awfully close to his head—she somehow knew they would not harm him.

Tsura peeked at David. He appeared to be dozing now, his fishing pole rigged between his knees in such a way that he would wake up should a fish decide to take the bait.

His questions about Eli were no more prying than the ones Gracie had plied her with since she first came to the farm. But she did not wish to talk about Eli. She had already told them all she ever would. He was gone. Bell too. And there was only her pup, Nellie, left to remind Tsura that life up to now had not been a dream.

Suddenly as Tsura gazed across the eddies, a mink glided across the stream, slipping out of the water within a couple of feet of the sycamore root. He raised up on his haunches and shook his sleek coat until the water stood out on it in oily beads. Then he turned back to gaze at the stream. Following the mink's gaze, Tsura saw that he was not watching the stream, but another mink trolling along the far bank. Without a sound, the second animal coasted into a narrow tributary, toward a small quiet delta where cattails grew in abundance. He dove under suddenly and vanished, leaving only a ripple as evidence that he'd been there at all.

Tsura reached over with her toe and bumped his leg. He opened his eyes, and she put her finger to her lips, motioning toward the first mink who still sat upright with his back turned to them, his gaze now focused on the spot where the second mink had been. And then, without warning, a familiar electric pain shot through Tsura's head. And in the next instant the sun grew brighter and flashed, a blinding white light behind her eyes. Her vision grew very sharp, very clear. She saw, not minks in a stream, but something else. She turned to look at him.

"David Busco," she said softly, "you will not go to the war."

14

SPRING PASSED, as it often did, in a sleight-of-hand way, infant leaves growing unnoticed until one day they were suddenly spread out over the trees in their full adult size, the pale, delicate chartreuse green of the hills quietly darkening by the hour into deep emerald maturity. Now it was June, and the timothy grass in the valley fields stood thick and lush, ready to cut.

Jess stood in the barn door one morning, watching the herd head out to graze. When the last cow had sauntered over the hill, hindquarters swaying, and dropped out of sight, he looked at his watch. Dawn was spreading pink over the dark horizon. The Busco boys would be driving in any minute. The day would be a long one. It promised to be hot and Jess was already out of sorts. Usually he looked forward to the fellowship of a haying crew. He especially liked having David and Lester with him in the fields, sharing the work. Today, though, he would be forced to divide his thoughts between work and worry, and that had him feeling edgy. So much that he had not had the patience, even, for Becky's plodding. He had turned her out with the cows. She had not gone, but lingered in the corral now, as if she hoped Jess would have a change of heart and harness her to the wagon.

It was Tsura. Gracie wanted her to stay on at the farm indefinitely. Permanently, it seemed. To her mind the thing was simple, as cut and dried as today's harvest of grass would soon be. She was, in fact, being uncharacteristically stubborn about it. The girl had sought shelter with them, she said, no one else, and that was reason enough to give it.

Jess was not so sure.

He could not deny feeling a kinship to Tsura—the girl was so much of the earth, so almost made of wind and sky and soil—but she was made of other stuff too. Material that was not of Jess's world. She disoriented him. And what he couldn't tell Gracie, not with her fondness for airing out rooms, was that almost since the day Tsura arrived, the place under his ribs he had thought was maybe filled, was at least sealed, had begun cracking open, revealing itself to be yet hollow. The girl was strangely keen. Her black gaze was a mirror, and Jess had no wish to see the man in it, haunted gray eyes peering back at him, the pale reflection of an inward, burrowing self. He sensed she had the power to suddenly unearth that man, naked as a mole, to the sun. It was unnerving, even alarming. No. He could not possibly accept Tsura as Gracie did, as a sister, or a daughter, or any other kind of foster kin. He wanted her away.

The boys came, and by seven-thirty Jess had them in the fields. Lester drove the truck pulling the hay wagon. Jess walked alongside, throwing bales up to David, who stacked them in ascending rows. David worked with quiet concentration, dovetailing the bales into tight-fitting stacks not likely to pitch. But he worked quickly too, always reaching for the next bale before Jess had hoisted it. Not much time had passed before Lester was bored with the job he'd chosen. Driving required less focus than stacking bales. He leaned his head out of the window.

"Saw a girl in the corral with your horse when we drove up, Jess," he called out.

"Did you?" Jess strode a few paces, squatted for a bale, and handed it up to David.

"You know we did," Lester said. "Who is she?"

"Well, she's a girl that until this summer lived in an old house up on Kerry Mountain. And now you know as much as I do."

Lester craned his neck to lean farther out, raising his voice so his brother would be sure to hear. "David thinks she's righteous."

"Now, how would he know that, just seeing her in the corral?"

"Don't go giving me the business, Jess. You're not that old," Lester said. He grinned, casting a sly look toward David, who ignored it. "He thinks she's a beauty."

"Ah. Well, he's right. She is that."

"I never said a word," David said, but his face, flushed already from sun and work, turned a deeper shade of red. He leaned down for the hay bale Jess was handing up. Hooking his fingers through the twine, he tossed it into a row, using his hip to drive it hard into an open slot.

Lester's eyes glinted with satisfaction.

Jess considered the brothers, soon to be parted by yet another war. He remembered Walter, and how much pleasure his brother had always got from deviling Clyde. Walter's easiness, his unworried ways, which Clyde perceived as indolence, had always run against their father's grain. Jess grinned, remembering the time his brother had memorized an entire poem for no more reason than orneriness.

Clyde had kept dozens of little moralizing verses in his memory—nicked from his farming quarterlies and used to motivate Walter. His favorite was the "Cheerful Plowman," a folksy rhyme expounding on the duties that make up a farmer's life, explaining what could happen if they were neglected or carried out in a poor, inadequate manner. Jess hated rhyming verse and had thought the poem dull, except for the last stanza, which always made him grin:

I once neglected fixing a neck yoke that was weak,
And soon my team was mixing with the fishes in the creek.

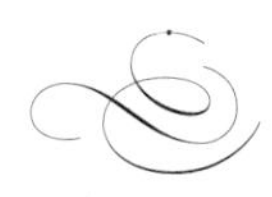

Walter had turned the tables on Clyde by perusing his collection of farming periodicals on the sly and filching a poem from *The Farm*

Implement News that suited his purpose. He stayed up late for several nights in a row, learning it. Because they shared a bedroom, Jess had been forced by consequence of proximity to learn it too. He could still recite it:

I'd like to be a boy again, without a woe or care,
with freckles scattered on my face and hayseed in my hair.

I'd like to rise at four o'clock and do a hundred chores
Like saw the wood and feed the hogs
and lock the stable doors.

And herd the hens and watch the bees
and take the mules to drink,
and teach the turkeys how to swim
so that they would not sink.

And milk about a hundred cows and bring in wood to burn,
and stand out in the sun all day
and churn and churn and churn.

And wear my brother's cast-off clothes
and walk four miles to school,
and get a licking every day for breaking some old rule,
and then go home again at night
and do the chores once more,
and milk the cows and slop the hogs
and feed the mules galore.

And then crawl wearily up the stairs to seek my little bed,
and hear Dad say, "That worthless boy!
He doesn't earn his bread!"

I'd like to be a boy again, a boy has so much fun,
his life is just one round of mirth,
from rise to set of sun.
I guess there's nothing pleasanter
than closing stable doors,
and herding hens and chasing bees
and doing evening chores.

Jess could almost hear, now, the light, mocking tone of Walter's voice as he sang the poem out in the darkness. He could feel, too, his own quiet contentment in those days, lying shirtless on top of the sheets on a hot summer's night, the windows open to ease the heat, safe in the knowledge that he could reach across the space, if need be, and touch his brother's arm for comfort.

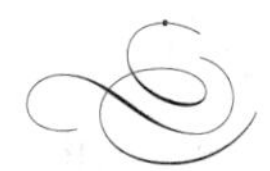

That evening, after the hay was all in, Jess and Gracie were sitting on the porch when Tsura walked up. She held out her hand to Gracie. There was a kitten cupped in her palm.

"That big white cat has moved her litter again," she said. "She left this one in the old nest. I tried to put it in the new one, but she rolled it back out."

"It's a runt," Jess said, in a tone that made him sound a lot like Clyde. "That mama cat likely knows there's something wrong. Better to leave well enough alone."

"There's nothing wrong with it," Tsura said firmly.

Jess looked sharply at her. From her expression he could see right away that she was not being contrary. It was only that she believed what she said to be fact, as if she *knew* the kitten had no malformity.

"Well, in that case," Gracie said, in a matter-of-fact voice, as if she too believed, "we'd better take care of the poor thing ourselves." She got up and went into the house. In a moment, she came back with a little glass doll's bottle. It had a rubber nipple, the right size for a kitten's mouth.

"Where did you get that?" Jess said, his tone turning harsh. He was irked now to anger. Gracie had been around barn cats long enough to know that nursing a discarded runt was a pointless endeavor. It was as if in Tsura's company she had gone under a spell. Now she was going to take the girl's word over her own good sense.

"I found it in the hall closet. It's been there since before my time. I guess I thought you knew about it."

Jess was quiet. He had remembered. The bottle went with a doll, the only survivor of the accident because it came sealed in a bubble of plastic. Why Millie, who had only grown sons, would have been carrying a doll around in her purse was a mystery to everyone, one never solved. More mysterious was why Jess had kept it. Death could make a man to do such peculiar things.

With no small amount of bitterness and with a great deal of reluctance, he did as Gracie bid and skimmed cream for the kitten at every milking for the next five days. The kitten ate greedily at every feeding. And by the time it was a week old, it had grown as big as any in the litter. Tsura snuck it back into the nest, and the big white cat began to nurse it along with the rest.

You could have knocked Jess down with a feather.

15

In the whole month of July, there was no rain. A drooth, the old valley women said, and Gracie did not think they exaggerated. There was an electric hum to everything. A big hot sun rose and burned ever and ever hotter through the day, parching all the flowers in her garden beds with thirst. Even the birds seemed to be waiting it out, their voices still and hushed, even at dawn. Why a dry summer should pass more slowly than any other kind, she did not know. She only knew that it was—passing far too slowly to suit a woman due to birth her first child at its end. She half believed it was only the rush and flow of the creek, the knowledge that if nowhere else than at the feet of Kerry Mountain water still lived, eternally pushing its way over and through the rocks, that kept her from losing her mind.

She stood in the dark, cool living room one afternoon, wondering if she could take it another minute, she was so hot and anxious. And then, as if to say, "Oh, yes, you can," Rose Marie's big station wagon unexpectedly pulled into the drive. Gracie was more than glad to have the distraction. She was shocked, though, to see her friend get out of the car alone and walk around the house to the kitchen door. Then she remembered Rose Marie mentioning over the phone that her brother had offered to take the Patterson children to the zoo in Pittsburgh. (Mike, Rose Marie had said, was playing the doting uncle to impress a woman he was hoping to make his latest wife.) Still it seemed to Gracie an odd, almost eerie sight, Rose Marie without a baby on her hip or a child in tow.

Tsura was in the yard. Gracie watched as she tossed a stick for Nellie to fetch. The dog was six months old now and brimful of pent-up energy. Already she had the temperament of a guard dog—which Jess thought she had very likely inherited from Prince, the Busco's German Shepherd—but had the open, friendly eyes and stately look of a collie, with her heavy brown coat and full, rough mane, streaked with white. She and Tsura, so tall and whittled, made a striking pair. Rose Marie turned her head to look at them as she passed, keeping an eye on the dog, whose ears and tail had stiffened. She gazed hard at the girl, who gazed serenely back. Gracie watched Rose Marie take in the whorled black thicket of hair that sheltered a wide, smooth forehead, the shape of her long, dark eyes. That beauty you could not deny and barely envied, if at all, it was that far beyond the ordinary.

"Does that girl remind you of anyone?" Rose Marie said, when she was inside. She sank into a chair and fanned herself with her pocketbook. She was winded and flushed from her walk around the house. As if she'd forgotten she'd already asked one question, she quickly posed another. "Feeling good?" she said.

"Feeling fat," Gracie said, smiling. She turned sideways, to show off her roundness.

"That's good," Rose Marie said with an approving nod. She shrugged out of her sweater, revealing a flamingo-pink and yellow plaid sundress.

"Fat is fine when it goes with happy. Me? I'm fat, but not so happy about it. Skip makes sure of that. And I suppose he's right. Sophie was three last month. Time I stopped eating for two. Problem is, after five babies in ten years, I'm not sure I remember how. Maybe I'd try, though, if he'd shut up about it." She sighed, shrugging her smooth brown shoulders. "You are so lucky to have married a quiet man. Sometimes I kick myself for introducing you two. If I'd had any sense, I'd have kept him for myself."

"I'm awfully glad you didn't," Gracie said with a smile.

"Speaking of, how is Jess?" Rose Marie said, and Gracie's smile fell away.

"What?" Rose Marie said, in a voice of mild alarm, her gaze now swift and searching. "What's wrong?"

"That's just it. I don't know what's wrong."

"Oh. Well, then." Rose Marie laughed, relieved. "You'd better assume nothing is."

"Maybe you're right," Gracie said, though she was not convinced. "But he isn't himself. He's too quiet, even for Jess. And he's been staying up far too late at night, reading his *Journals*.

"Journals?" Rose Marie's brow scrunched into a puzzled knot. "What sort of journals?"

"Of Lewis and Clark," Gracie said, raising her voice. The tea kettle had begun its tuneless whistle. She went to the stove, took it off the flame, and poured the tea, leaving it to steep. She came back to the table. Rose Marie still looked puzzled.

"That's how he settles his mind," Gracie said. "He's done it since he was a boy. So I know something is troubling him."

"That is an odd method for soothing nerves." Rose Marie said. "But less risky than liquor, I suppose."

Gracie turned, reaching for cups hanging from pegs on the wall behind her.

At the sight of the cups, Rose Marie laughed and shook her head. "You can't offer me hot tea on a day like this, Gracie. I'm Sicilian, remember, not Russian." She rose and went to the cabinet, found a tumbler, and went over to the icebox, opening the freezer door.

"My God, it's an ice factory in here," she said. "Six, no seven trays." She took one out and pulled the lever. The ice in the tray cracked into cubes. "At my house, they'd all be empty. Every single one."

Gracie laughed, a low, absent chuckle. She was focused on a tightening across her middle. When the baby had got settled again, head down, she could feel a sharp new protrusion through the fabric of her light cotton smock, the small, pointed knob of a knee, or a tiny elbow. She caressed it dreamily. One day, and she could hardly wait for it, she was going to open her own freezer door and find that a child had put the ice tray back empty.

"Don't worry too much about Jess," Rose Marie said, seating herself back at the table. "He's scared and trying to hide it. That's all."

"What do you mean?"

"Ducks and cats."

Gracie tilted her head, her expression quizzical.

"See," Rose Marie said, "when it comes to starting a family, I always think that women are ducks and men are cats. Both can swim. But the cat's not nearly so keen on jumping into the water, or as natural-looking doing it."

"I suppose," Gracie said, doubtful. "But Jess likes to swim. And he's good at it. He's going to be fine as a father. Any man who will break a horse as gently he does will be good with a child. You know that better than me. He doted on you. And he was only a boy then. No, there's something else. I sense it. And it seems as if it started with Tsura. He didn't want to let her stay, you know. I had to talk him into it."

"That's a twist," Rose Marie said, with a wry look. "If a girl that lovely and seventeen showed up at my door, I'd be escorting her to the sidewalk. But, then again, I'm not married to Jess Hazel. He never was one to look around much, even before you. And he sure wasn't after."

"I might feel as you say, if she were any other attractive girl," Gracie said quietly, keeping her eyes on her tea. The wistfulness in Rose Marie's voice had brought forth a forgotten image: Skip, on the night of his and Rose Marie's wedding, dancing a bridesmaid into a dark corner, his hand sliding smoothly down from the girl's waist to rest on the soft, intimate curve of her lower hip. And though she knew it couldn't have been the song that was playing, she heard a rasping voice, the plaintive lament: *Lord, a good man is hard to find.* "But Tsura isn't just a lovely girl," she said lightly, to cover the small, quick ache knotting in her chest. "She's a lovely soul. There's something good and pure in her, almost saintly. It draws you in and soothes you in the most natural way, like one of those hot mineral springs people bathe in for healing. You'll know it the minute you meet her."

Rose Marie looked unimpressed, even skeptical. "Maybe," she shrugged. "Maybe not. I'm still passing for Catholic, but there are days when I doubt there was ever any such thing as a saint. And if there was, I have a feeling they've gone extinct now. To tell the truth, if it weren't for knowing you, I'm not sure I could believe in souls at all, much less one that's naturally good and pure, like you say."

"You sound like Jess," Gracie said. "He just finds her odd. And that's too bad," she added slyly. "Because I think she hears from angels. But we can talk about something else."

16

JESS GREW MORE AND MORE UNSURE, as the days went by, that he could take much more of Tsura. Very often while guiding Becky through a field or settling himself under a cow, he would go over in his mind what he would say to convince Gracie. He never got far.

"I want her gone," he would say, and Gracie would go into early labor, putting an end to the discussion.

The girl wasn't going anywhere. He just had to accept it, find a way to deal with it. But the closer Gracie's due date grew, the closer to the house Tsura stayed. She had stopped her wild roaming with Nellie through the woods and berry canes. Quit too her habit of heading to cool her feet in the old spring house or going down to wade Muddy Creek in the heat of the afternoon. She was always underfoot now. Haunting Gracie, it seemed to Jess, and increasing his own disquiet.

"Son, you're tight as a drawn bow," Pat Badger said when Jess ran smack into him at the Feed & Seed.

Which, looking back, Jess could see was about the rightest statement Pat ever made.

PART FOUR

1

IN THE SECOND WEEK OF SEPTEMBER, Jess awakened with a start. Nellie's wet nose brushed against his hand. She whined a little. He and Gracie were sleeping in the first-floor bedroom. The baby was a week overdue, and climbing the stairs made Gracie's legs swell.

The bedroom had been Clyde and Millie's. Jess still felt strange sleeping in the folks' big wrought-iron bed.

He lay with his eyes open to the darkness, orienting himself. Though he could not see it, he knew there was an overnight case sitting under the window straight ahead, crosswise from the bedpost. It seemed ages since he had watched Gracie pack it. Inside were pajamas strewn with tiny yellow flowers, a robe, slippers, a tube of toothpaste and a toothbrush, the Pond's night cream she never went to bed without, her hairbrush, and a miniature double-faced icon fitted with tiny brass hinges, so it could be stood on a table or folded up and stored away. The little suitcase, all packed, latched, and ready to go, had seemed so hopeful then, so expectant. Like Gracie.

Jess comforted himself with the knowledge that everything was all right, for only the day before Doc had reassured them that Gracie's due date wasn't set in stone. He said it was perfectly normal for a first baby, for any baby, to be late by a week.

"Maybe so," Gracie had said irritably to Jess when Doc was out of earshot. "But by my estimations, this one is late by two."

Nellie whined again, more insistent, just as Jess was dozing off. He sat up this time, coming fully awake. The hands on the clock glowed green. It was 2:15. When Nellie had last been let out before chore time, she had disturbed a nest of skunks.

"Upstairs," he hissed, pushing her away with his hand.

Nellie didn't move. He glanced at Gracie. She was sleeping soundly, rolled onto her left side with her back to him, belly resting on the mattress. Jess got reluctantly to his feet. He climbed the stairs with Nellie on his heels, leading her back to Tsura's room—the small alcove bedroom at the end of the hall where Millie had always done her sewing. When the baby was big enough to move from cradle to crib, Gracie had said, just last night, then Tsura could take the big room downstairs, and the little sewing room could become a nursery. It had given Jess a bad feeling when Gracie said that. But whether the feeling sprang from the notion of Tsura living in Clyde and Millie's old room or the realization that Gracie still intended her stay to be permanent, he couldn't tell.

At the top of the stairs, he could see that the door to the girl's room stood wide. The covers had been thrown back, and the bed was empty. A cold, inexplicable fear seized Jess's chest when he saw it. He turned and almost ran down the stairs. As he came through the door of the bedroom, he could see, in the dim light from the upstairs hall, a small white figure. It was Tsura, he realized wildly in the next second. And the sight of her standing in her long nightgown over Gracie, like some ghostly spirit of the night, confounded Jess's mind, even as it angered him. He did not know if she had been in the room all the time or if she had somehow managed to reach it first without crossing his path. However she had managed it, one thing was certain. She had no business being there at all.

Gracie lay on her side as he had left her, in a deep sleep. No, Jess realized then, and his heart stumbled. Everything was wrong. Gracie slept lightly by trait. She should have been awake long before now, wondering why Nellie was moaning and what he and Tsura were doing milling about the house. He reached out with a trembling hand and touched her hair, her arm, her face. She lay still. Jess's legs buckled. His breath felt hot and dry. He thought he might be sick. He tore back the bedclothes in a quick, feverish movement and shouted her name. She was so still. Too still. He groped her form, feeling his way along it in the darkness with blind hands, as if he did not know it inch for inch. He barked at Tsura to turn on the light. The old push-button switch clicked and the overhead light flashed on, cruel and bright, revealing the room too suddenly. Tsura cried out, a small, stark wail. Gracie lay as still as glass, the thin material of her gown wrapped tightly around her legs and swollen torso. Her skin shone a pale, translucent gray. Jess whirled away, headed for the telephone. But when Tsura cried out again, he paused, glancing back. Gracie lay as still as ever. Tsura pointed to her nightgown, shifting of its own accord. Jess froze half-turned in the doorway, gazing at the scene in the bed. A salt statue, he would later think, watching helplessly over his shoulder as his life was reduced to ash. The nightgown twitched again, then moved in a slow, taut wave across Gracie's belly as the baby changed positions.

Jess ran to the phone in earnest then, and when Doc had been called and the ambulance was on the way, he ran back into the bedroom, only to see Tsura making a strange motion with her hand over the length of the bed. Later, when his senses returned, it would dawn on him that she was only trying to help Gracie and the baby, signing them with a cross, the way Gracie had likely taught her to do. It would be days, though, before Jess would recall anything about the moment—before he would even think of Tsura again. Now, standing over his wife, the girl seemed a dark, dread messenger, the spirit of old doom. And Jess came undone.

2

A SLOW NIGHTMARE BEGAN. Jess went out on the porch to watch for the ambulance. Soon it came shrieking down the lane with red lights flashing, a grotesque sight against the dark, quiet hills, and as it pulled up in front of the house, the door was already opening. "Where is she?" Doc shouted as he rolled out. He heaved his bulk quickly up the steps and followed Jess into the house.

Inside, Doc headed for the stairs. "Not there," Jess said, and took him by the arm, led him into the bedroom. But the sight of his wife, so pale and small and still, shocked him all over again. The words he had been about to speak froze on his tongue. Doc didn't need them anyway. He was already feeling for Gracie's pulse, his jaw set at a grim angle. Sickness rose in Jess's throat. He turned sharply on his heel and left the room.

When the ambulance medics entered, Jess showed them to the door of the bedroom, but declined to enter. He closed the door to the room and brought a chair from the kitchen, then sat down to wait in the hall, preferring the terror of the unknown to what he might chance to see. His heart had gone wild, beating all out of time, unnerved as he was to the point of exhaustion. Too many nights he had knelt in the darkness to aid an animal in trouble. He had no doubt the situation in the bedroom was a grave one.

A sudden gust of warm wind blew in through the open living room windows, lifting the curtains in two white wings. Gracie was human. And, as she'd once said of Zook, she had all the usual frailties and weakness. Sins, she called them, without flinching. But Jess knew she did not fear death. Not as he did. She was as unmoved by the winds of doubt as Kerry Mountain. The valley and the farm and all that she cherished on the good earth paled next to the kingdom of heaven. And for the first time since he was a boy, Jess wished in anguish to own such certainty. With it, he felt he might pray. As it was, he could only groan.

There was a sound of activity in the bedroom, then the low, rough rumble of Doc's voice giving orders, and a scraping, as if the bed were being scooted across the floor. And in the next instant, a baby's small, furious cry. Minutes later, Doc strode out carrying the baby, bundled in his white coat. The medics followed behind with the gurney. Jess leaped to his feet, his eyes searching beyond the men to the figure they carried. They walked quickly past, hurrying the gurney down the steps and into the ambulance. Jess caught a bare, fleeting glimpse of Gracie's still form, covered with a sheet, and Doc's mouth, a bleak, gray slash, as he said, "Best follow in your own truck, Jesse."

3

AT THE HOSPITAL, Jess sat stricken and numb in the hall while the hospital doctor spoke in hushed tones to him of what he already knew. Gracie was gone. In a daze, he got up, went to the water fountain, and pushed the button down with his thumb. After a moment, he took his thumb away and turned around, having no idea if he had taken a drink. Anyway, he wasn't thirsty. He saw Rose Marie coming down the hall toward him. She looked as haggard as he felt. Blue eye shadow streaked across her lids, her false lashes looked as though she had glued them on in the dark, and her hair had not been set. He wondered when she had dyed her curls that brassy red shade and thought it didn't suit her.

"Hey, Rose Marie," he said.

"Hey," she said, hugging his waist. "I just came from the nursery." She gave a tiny smile. "I got to hold her. They're amazed, you know, by how healthy she is, considering. They're calling it a miracle. We're all calling it a miracle," she said, reaching for his hand.

Jess had no reply to that. He took his hand away. Rose Marie shook her head, pressing her lips tightly together.

"Is it what they're saying? A heart defect?"

"I guess," Jess said, dully. "That's what Doc believes. He says it's rare, but he has seen it once or twice. A malformed valve. She would have had it since birth. But we won't know without an autopsy."

"Is there going to be an autopsy?"

"Probably not. Darya has a big problem with it. And for once, I think we agree on something. I don't want anyone . . . It just wouldn't help. Knowing isn't going to bring her back."

"No, of course not. I hate to talk about such hard things so soon, Jess, but there are going to be decisions to make. I'm here to help if you want me to, but let the Morozovs in, will you? Being Russian, there may be customs—things they do that we don't, or that we do and they don't. Anyway, they're taking this very hard. Just try and remember, if you can, that they've lost her too."

Jess watched her until she reached the door. He sighed, turning away. His knees felt weak, and he was lightheaded.

4

JESS OBEDIENTLY DID as Rose Marie said. He brought the Morozovs into the funeral plans. The truth was that he handed them over completely. There was to be no embalming. According to their custom, Gracie's own mother would wash and dress her body, and Ivan and Jess would fashion from wood—pine, or perhaps cedar—the casket in which she would be laid. She would then be taken to the church, where a psalter vigil would be kept until the next morning, when Father Antony would perform the funeral service. Jess felt sure the arrangements were just as Gracie would have wished. Nothing that was proposed surprised him. There was even some relief in it. He could not have borne to send Gracie off from a funeral parlor like the one that had buried his folks, anyway—could not have stood again, even for an hour, another pale, hunched mortician with a moist handshake and a familiar way of speaking of someone else's dead. Nor did he believe his warm-hearted wife would have rested easily in a cold, metal coffin.

As the hours passed and the time for Gracie's burial approached, Jess found that the thing which gripped him was no ordinary sadness. That grief he was familiar with. It held a seed of hope, for it came marked by a season. The mourning period. You endured for a time, and then you brought your grieving to an end, much to the relief of others. Jess sensed that this was something else. This was a sorrow without season, without end. One to abide with. Perhaps forever.

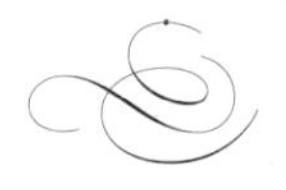

Three days later, Gracie rested in the triple-domed shadow of Holy Transfiguration Church, her grave marked in the Russian way, by a white three-bar cross. Along the road to the churchyard cemetery, the goldenrod was in glorious blaze, and Jess could hardly bear to see it. Gracie had so loved to walk along the gold-topped fencerows in autumn. And he had always thought she mingled so naturally with that wildflower, moving in her gentle way among the slender waving stalks.

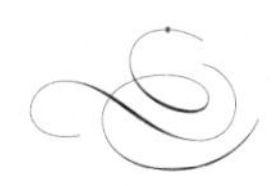

It was a well-attended funeral. And a lovely memorial, more than one person who was there later told Jess. A beautiful, ancient rite. Prayers that made it seem as if Gracie spoke on behalf of her own soul. Very moving, they said. But Jess had little memory of it. He would at odd moments smell faintly the odors of myrrh and frankincense, hear snatches of something that had been chanted in English—all things are vanity, and life is but a shadow . . . in the sweetness of Thy beauty, O Christ, give rest to her whom Thou hast chosen—and he would see Darya bending her face to Gracie's for a last kiss. But even then—despite the proper smells, the appointed prayers, the scenes that all told him the funeral had taken place in reality—his memory would have a vagueness to it, as if he had stumbled into another man's dream.

He did recall vividly a church packed with friends and loved ones, many of them faces he hadn't seen since his and Gracie's wedding. Rose Marie was there of course, and Mike, with Pop and Rita. The Buscos had come, all four. And Gracie's nuns, in robes the color of mourning. Even Pat Badger was there in the church, with Peggy. And once they were graveside, Jess remembered, Pat had laid an arm across Jess's back. They'd stayed that way during the entire, mercifully brief burial service, Pat squeezing his shoulder in a painful grip. And when Father Antony had nodded to David and Lester, who had helped carry the coffin and had then stood by to fill the grave, Jess had listened dry-eyed for the all-too-familiar sound, steeling his heart as the first shovelful of earth rained down. With each awful thud, Darya sobbed.

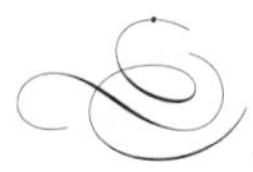

That evening, when all the people had gone, and Jess could be alone with his sorrow, he went back to the cemetery. He walked slowly down the hill, winding through the forest of crosses, his stomach twisted into a knot of dread. And then, just below the second rise, he saw it. The grave mound. As he drew near, he could smell the fresh, raw earth and the perfume of the funeral flowers—fragile hothouse stems set into blocks of hard green foam, arranged over the grave in groups to hide the dirt. They were meant to soothe, he knew, to soften a harsh truth, but they did not manage it. The truth was bitterer for the pretense. He moved a little closer then and saw lying on a bare patch near the foot of the grave a sturdy spray of goldenrod. And for the first time since Gracie's death, he remembered Tsura. She had often brought to Gracie wildflowers picked on her wanderings. He had to acknowledge, if vaguely, his heart too heavy with grief to bear the added weight of guilt, that it must have been Tsura who had brought the goldenrod, forced because of him to steal to Gracie's grave in secret.

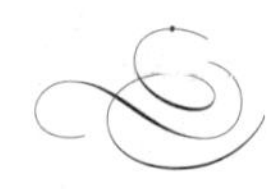

Gracie's folks came out of the house when Jess got home, to watch him come down the lane. They stood very close, Darya leaning into Ivan. Seen from a distance, the pair made a single forlorn figure. Jess swung left at the split and pulled the truck below the barn. He had no wish to mingle his pain with theirs. There was no denying the help they had been since that terrible night. He couldn't have done it without them. But it was a damned uncomfortable arrangement, to say the least.

5

IN THE WEE HOURS, Jess heard the scream of a barn owl. He rose from his chair and went to the open window, pulling back the curtain to peer out into the darkness. The night had been warm, but the air was cool now that dawn approached. A breeze blew in, lifting his hair and the fabric of his shirt. He gazed into the bassinet at his feet, at the swaddled baby. Darya had bound her in a cocoon of blankets, tighter than a Chinese foot. He looked out the window again, watched as the owl flew in on silent wings and landed on the near edge of the barn roof. There was a pale full moon, casting enough light that Jess could see a small animal pinned in the owl's talons. A vole, most likely, snatched up from the corral floor where rodents often gleaned the manure piles for kernels of undigested grain. The vole struggled mightily in the bird's grasp. The owl bent its head to the animal, then gazed away, as if contemplating mercy. Jess had traveled little, other than vicariously in books. Still, if there existed on earth an eerier creature than the common barn owl, all ghost-faced and hollow-eyed, he would need to see it for proof. He had seen birds of prey with their bounty enough times to know there would be no reprieve for the vole. He dropped the curtain and went back to his chair.

Just then the baby stirred in her cradle and began to fret a little. Jess tensed. She fussed quietly, tiny kittenish sounds, then fell silent, but Darya had caught the noise. Her sigh drifted out of the open bedroom door. She shuffled heavily out, snapping her robe together as she walked, and went directly into the kitchen. Jess heard the stove knob click to pilot, heard the gas lighting, the faucet running, and a pan being set on the stove. In a little while, she came into the living room holding a bottle and sat down in Gracie's chair. She squeezed a few drops of liquid from the nipple onto the inside of her wrist. Then she held the bottle out to Jess, shaking it at him a couple of times to indicate he should take it. Reluctantly, Jess took the bottle, and set it on his knee. Darya closed her eyes. She slept immediately, breathing deeply through her nose. The baby slept too, her chest rising and falling almost imperceptibly with each breath. A cloud passed over the moon and lingered. Jess turned his face away, unable to gaze any longer at Gracie's child, cradled in a basket instead of her arms. She would have been a natural too. Would have taken to mothering with the same ease she had taken to loving, assuming with Jess a teacherly stance, as if being born a woman made her a shade or two less green. He laid a hand over his heart. To ease the ache.

In the dim light, everything in the room spoke to him of Gracie. Under the window were her begonias, a multigenerational family, rooted cuttings shuttled off often to live and multiply under other windows in other homes. At the far end of the divan, her knitting basket still held a skein of yellow yarn and a tiny, half-finished hat. The cloth-draped icons on the shelf in the corner, though, proclaimed her best. There was the true center of her life, the hub on which the entire wheel of it turned. The dark-eyed saints, so kind to Gracie, gazed severely at Jess, offering him scant comfort.

Suddenly the baby cried out, piercing the silence with a fit of frantic, rhythmic screams. Darya got heavily to her feet and reached into the cradle, grunting. Jess fumbled for the bottle. Darya set the baby on her shoulder with one hand, ignoring her cries, and reached with the other into the basket on the floor beside the cradle for a diaper. In what seemed a single swift movement, she had slipped off the wet napkin and pinned on the dry one. She swaddled the baby again and handed her, still screaming, to Jess.

"Time for milk," she said, nodding toward the bottle. Jess pulled his knees together and laid the baby in the trough of his lap, aiming the nipple at her mouth.

"Nyet," Darya said, pulling her eyebrows into a frown. She made a little cradling motion with her arms.

Jess handed the baby back to her.

"You do it," he said.

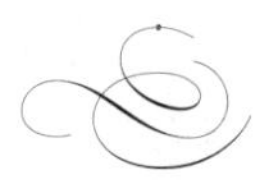

Dawn came at last, with Jess still awake and fully dressed. He rose and made coffee, taking it into the living room to drink. It was just too much to ask of himself, to sit in the cold, dark kitchen, knowing Gracie was never again going to come shuffling into it half-asleep and offer him breakfast. He could not see the barn from the front window, only the tip of the weathervane jutting out of the mist. A front had rolled in overnight. The air was cool and the fog hung thick, blanketing the farm beneath. He drained his cup, hardly tasting the coffee, and took it to the sink. On the back porch, he shrugged into a jacket and walked outside. From over the hill, he could hear the low of the cows, bawling out their insecurity. A lonesome sound in the fog-soaked valley. There was a clinking of boot buckles. Ivan materialized out of the gloom, steam rising off the wash bucket he carried. Neither spoke. Jess turned, and they walked together down the hill to the barn.

They worked in silence, each focused on his task. Jess filled the troughs with feed, then went up to the front of the barn to tend to other chores while Ivan washed down the udders and any soiled areas that might dirty the milk. When the cows had been washed, Jess returned and met Ivan in the middle of the row. He set a bucket under Ivan's cow, then seated himself on his own stool, the one his father had made for him, with the legs knocked off short to ease his back. The milking shed was cold still, so early in the morning and it being on the shaded side of the barn, but neither Jess nor Ivan searched for gloves. The warmth of the udder was enough to limber stiff fingers. Jess had no idea why Ivan milked without gloves—he'd never asked. As for himself, he milked barehanded for the same reason he didn't use machines: the pure pleasure of it. More than once he'd considered crossing over, watching cows get milked by suction at the fair, but in the end always decided against it. No one was getting out of this thing alive, anyhow, whether he kept to the old way like the Amish, or went the new, making constant, and costly, changes. And if neither way was going to be the salvation of a farm like Hazel Valley, the second had at present a taint of foolishness. As there was an agreeable symbiosis in the old way—the cow quietly letting down her milk, you easing her of it with your own clean, bare hands—and Jess could see none of that in the loud, too-eager suckling of the machines at the fair, he was glad to have a good, sound excuse (what decision could be saner than one that made financial sense?) for not asking his cows to endure it.

He happened to glance down the row just then and saw that Ivan sat forward on his stool with his hand lifted, three fingers pressed together as if holding a pen or pencil. As Jess watched, the man drew, in a long, slow, deliberate motion of his hand, an invisible cross of blessing over his cow's flanks. The sight brought a sudden sweet sadness to Jess's chest, for he knew that had Gracie been seated on the stool, she would have made the same gesture. Ivan was reaching his hands toward the udder now, murmuring soft, tender encouragements to the cow, a skittish, first-calf heifer who was rolling her eye at him. Ivan's behavior was almost quaint, taken on its own. But the meekness in it, at a time when a man might have been excused for being impatient or even cruel, took Jess completely by surprise. He'd never witnessed such honest, uncontrived humility. It struck him, oddly, as a thing of grave beauty. Pat Badger often went on in his modest way about the sacredness to be found in the things of earth, about how driving a post or shoeing a horse could become an act of worship. But Ivan wasn't talking—he was doing, filling the barn with his old-man love.

Jess had never wanted so much to weep.

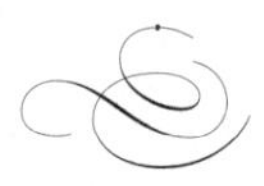

He dozed fitfully in his chair that night, dreaming of Gracie. In the dream he stood beside their bed, gazing down on her. She was whole and slim, but fragile in some new way, her flesh both brittle and translucent, as if she wore an onion's skin. She was holding the baby out to Jess, urging him to take her. In the way of dreams, once Jess had taken the baby, she changed in his arms and became Tsura. Gracie rose from the bed, bent to the child in Jess's arms, and blessed her, signing the cross. Then she led Jess to the cradle, motioning to it with her hand, as if to say that he should place Tsura in it. Jess readily obeyed, for Tsura had become burdensome, growing heavier and heavier in his arms as he dreamed. But what Jess saw when he went to lay her in the cradle caused him to recoil, for it was not a cradle. It was a casket. He held Tsura tighter to his chest and backed away from it, turning in fear to Gracie. She was gone.

6

NEXT MORNING, as soon as his work was done, Jess drove up Kerry Mountain to Zook's house. There was no answer when he knocked, which came as a shock to Jess. Somehow, he had not imagined Tsura would not be here, on the mountain. He poked around the yard a little before trying the back door. He found it unlocked and went in. The place was spartan. The kitchen was large and sun-washed white, the only furnishings a wood-burning stove, a pump-handle sink, and a plain oak table with two straight-backed chairs. There were no dirty dishes in the sink or trash in the bin. No sign of recent living. The only evidence of Tsura at all Jess found in the attic, under the bed in what must have been her room. It was a small rosewood box, carved in flowers and leaves. In it were a couple of blue bird feathers, a tiny piece of fossilized wood, and a tuft of fur from a rabbit's nest. Jess fingered each item gently, thinking how very unstrange they were, the sort of treasures any child might secret away. Then, as he went to close the lid, he saw there was something tucked into it. It was a photo. Or rather, it was half a photo, torn neatly down the center. And staring out of it, grinning for all he was worth in black and white, was Walter.

7

THE PHOTO HEAPED COALS on Jess's head. What had been a kind of vague remorse now gave way to real contrition. "And don't we all sin?" Jess heard Gracie say. Well, yes, he admitted now, if you had to put it that way, so stark and blunt, he did. As did Clyde. And so, in her glancing-down way, did Millie.

It was a hard thing to accept.

He was coming to see that the path to truth was not a path at all, but a rugged mountain road, high and lonesome and winding, and when you had rounded any kind of sharp bend, or finally crested a hill, there was only yourself to meet.

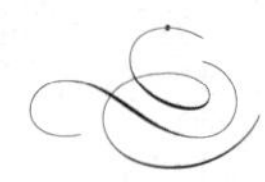

Not two days later, Jess ran into Pat Badger at the Feed & Seed. Pat was examining a bright-yellow nylon bridle. He had it stretched tight across a wide space between his large hands, testing its strength.

"What do you think of these, Jesse? Have you used 'em?"

"I have," Jess said. "I guess I think they're all right. But," he grinned, "you know how Becky can be, so stuck in her ways. When I asked if she'd like to trade her old leather bridle, worn soft as a dog's ear, for a fancy nylon one like you've got there, she said no, she didn't think so, but thanks just the same."

Pat laughed. He hung the bridle back on the hook. They went outside and stood, each with a hand on the bed of Pat's truck, making small talk. And then, almost naturally, as if the farrier were a priest Jess had asked to hear his confession, he found himself unburdening, telling Pat all about the fit of blind anger he'd been in on the night of Gracie's death, how he had all but thrown Tsura bodily out of the house.

"Lord, Pat, I was all out of my mind. I don't remember what I said. I hardly remember doing it at all, but it must have been terrible for her. I was hoarse from it, couldn't talk in a right voice for days."

"Aye," was all Pat said. But it was a good reply, for while the old bygone word could not absolve a wrong, it yet blessed and said a man was understood. Jess went on to tell him, then, about the photo and how the halves fit like two pieces of an old puzzle, and how he thought he knew now what Clyde had done to break Millie's heart. Strangely enough, as Jess talked of this, a bright spot of rhubarb color appeared at the base of Pat's thick neck and began unfurling like the tendrils of a fern over his throat until it reached his ears, flushing them scarlet. Jess watched in discomfort, his own face reddening. He had never known Pat to be ill at ease. He said, quietly "You knew about this."

"Yes and no," Pat said. "I knew there weren't many wives could do what Millie did. What she wanted to do, rather. It was Clyde who wasn't having it. Wouldn't own up to anything."

"I know that," Jess said. "It's just what I've been saying."

"No, son. You're not taking my meaning."

"Well, say it so I can then," Jess said, irritably. He was getting a bad feeling.

Pat balked. "No," he said, and slapped his leg with the flat of his hand. He shook his head. "It was May Day. There may have been spirits afoot. And I had only her word to go on. To be sure, labor pain is a truth serum. Peg got all kinds of honest when she was having our boys, told me a great many things about myself I didn't necessarily want to know."

"That's no answer, and you know it," Jess said.

A look of patience came into Pat's blue eyes and he said, quietly, slowly, "You've been fussing over your father a long time, Jesse. You've combed his hair and fixed his tie straight until he's looking right smart. Good enough to bury. What say we do it? And let him rest in peace."

Jess put his hands in his pockets, looked off down the road where a car was just rounding the curve.

Not expecting a reply, of course, Pat went on: "The pale truth is that however Tsura came to be in the world, and whoever it was should have been raising her, it was Eli Zook who did. There was wisdom in his ways too. He made a fine nest there on the mountain, grew up a splendid little swallow bird, and left her free to fly and perch as she pleased. None of us could have done near so well. Not for her."

"Pretty high praise for a man you told me you couldn't vouch for."

"I also told you he was a friend," Pat said coolly. "Eli has spells. Times when his mind can't just simmer—it must boil. And once the pot has run clean over, he sinks into a cold, dark place and stays there for days. What I didn't know until Tsura was old enough to fend for herself is that there are times when he takes off, leaves the mountain." He paused, and when he continued Jess caught a tinge of regret, even remorse, in his voice. "She begs me not to grieve too much on it. Says a woman with sad, sweet eyes always came to stay in the house when Eli was gone, a story I'll admit gives me trouble. But I am in no way saying it isn't true. Anyhow, after a day or two, he makes his way back home. This last time, he just didn't do that. Didn't come back."

"Any idea where he is?"

"None. Until last week. That's when Tsura told me she'd seen him. You know, *seen*, in her way. She said he was with the Amish and wouldn't be coming home to the mountain. So I did some checking with the ones I know. She's right," he said, and there was no mistaking the catch of sorrow in his voice. "Zook won't be back to these parts."

"Why not?" Jess asked quietly, already sure of the answer.

"Well, because he's dead. Must have been just before Tsura showed up in your barn last winter, he took off from the mountain one night and walked all the way to New Wilmington. Some folks on a tour bus spied him the next morning, sitting on the rise of the hill above the highway. Had his arm around his dog and his eyes wide open, staring across the road at his sister's house. Being unfamiliar with Amish ways, they thought he was a statue, placed on the hillock for them to gawk at. Frozen stiff is what he was, of course. It was dead, bitter cold. Whether he meant to go that way, nobody can know now. But I think not."

"Because he wouldn't have walked all that way to die?"

"Because he wouldn't leave Tsura."

"But he did leave her."

"Yes," Pat said, and the patience in his voice sounded tried, as if he had begun to doubt Jess's ability to understand a plain and simple thing, "but only in the way I just said. The wandering-off way. He didn't know it would be for good."

Jess said stubbornly, "You can't be sure. Not if he's dead."

"I am, though," Pat insisted. "I delivered Tsura. I witnessed her first breath. I brought the priest that baptized her. And I brought him again, and the coroner, when her mother died. Helped Eli dig Maria's grave. I've watched him look after Tsura like a daughter for eighteen years. As I said, he did go off moon-crazy every now and again, and I've no doubt that was hard on her. Harder, I'm sure, than you or I will ever know. But he never lifted a hand to hurt her. I'd stake all I have on that belief. And he wouldn't have left her for the world."

8

THROUGH AN OPENING IN THE TREES, Tsura could see the cross on the bell tower. The chapel was lit. She crept closer until she could hear the quiet, blended singing of the nuns. "O Gladsome Light." They were praying Vespers. It was only just now falling dusk, but for them tomorrow had already begun.

The song pierced Tsura's heart. She tried to remember the story Gracie had told her about how it first came to be sung long ago, when there was a light that burned always in the tomb of Christ. It saddened her that she could not remember all of the story. It was always that way when Gracie had talked to her of church. The stories and explanations sparked her mind but wouldn't stay put so that she could recall them later. What did stay was this warmth she felt in the nearness of the nuns, the sweetness of their prayer. Like water from a secret mountain spring, she had begun to crave it.

She listened, hidden in the brush, until the service ended, then turned and walked in dimming light back into the woods, to the cool, shallow cave where she was camped. Tomorrow, because she had promised, she would go with David Busco to see the falls at Hell's Hollow. An image flashed before her then. And for the first time in her life, her spirit balked at the knowledge pressed upon it. She was suddenly weary of seeing.

"How long?" she asked, even as she yielded.

She lit the lantern and reached into the bag she had found left for her in the hollowed oak at the edge of the woods. Then she heard it. Below the urgent roiling of the nearby creek. Under the secretive, gathering rustle of the forest night. The voice. So familiar. Small and still and soft as the moon shining through the branches of the trees.

A little longer, child.

Always the same answer. Because, she knew, it was the only answer. But hearing it, she was at peace. She ate two of Darya's rye and onion sandwiches, readied her pallet, put out the lantern, and lay down in the darkness to sleep.

9

THE NEXT DAY, driving the milk to the cheese factory, Jess arrived, having been absent in mind for most of the journey. His conversation with Pat had shone a little light on the situation with Tsura. And if the beam was a narrow one, stingy and slanting, it was enough to harden Jess's resolve, make fast his need to find her and do all he could to set things right.

The night before at dinner, Darya had finally confessed that she knew Tsura was living in the woods along Muddy Creek, near Zodie and Orville's old place, near the spot at Mill Bend where Gracie's nuns had built their new monastery; and now Jess was worried in earnest. Not that Tsura wasn't just fine sleeping in the forest. She was as much so as a deer, and the weather was warm because of the late Indian summer. But there were rumors of vagabonds in the valley. Travelers, Pat called them. Hippies, Rose Marie said. Whatever anyone called them, they were young folks journeying across the land in packs, boys and girls together, pitching their tents at night in the valley fields. They were making their way slowly west from a bohemian gathering in New York. Jess thought that if any stopped on his land, he would allow them to stay a short while, as Margit Busco had always let the gypsies do—as Jess had always wished his father would do too. Why not? So long as they stayed to fallow ground and tended properly to their fires. But he didn't want Tsura stumbling into their midst. She was a clever girl in her own way, but she had never even read a newspaper, could have no knowledge of the world these travelers would have seen.

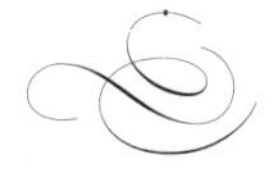

There was a line already in front of the delivery door, two wagons and two pickup trucks. Jess would have to wait his turn to unload. The Amish team horses fidgeted nervously in their harnesses while the drivers carried on a conversation in their brand of German. Even with the rumble of the idling truck engines, Jess could hear their companionable tone. When his turn came, he set his milk cans out, lining them up on the loading dock. Just as he finished, Jakob Miller, the factory foreman, came out to the truck in his apron. He didn't bother with small greetings, didn't mention the morning fog, didn't bring up the unusually warm autumn weather. He laid his hand on the bedrail of the truck, staring off toward the road.

"You want your payment now, Jesse?" he said.

Jess tried to remember a single moment in all the years he'd been selling milk to the cheese factory when Jakob Miller had looked him in the eye. There wasn't one that he could bring to mind.

"No need to pay me now," he said. "You can just mail it to the house. Same as always."

"I have some news, Jesse," Jakob said. "Not such good news."

Jess laughed. "What could be so bad, Jakob? I'm already selling you Grade A milk for a B price. You've got something worse than that?"

Jakob's forehead knotted under the brim of his hat. He looked down, as if examining the leather toes of his boots. "Yah. I do," he said soberly. "You know since they quit hauling milk out of Portersville, there's been too much coming in here, with all the little farms needing somewhere to go with it. Now I gotta cut back. Hazel milk is clean, and you been selling here a long time, so I'm only cutting you to two days. The others is gonna get one."

Jakob was right. This was bad news. But Jess had known worse. And thanks to his change-wary Hazel blood, he had been checking the winds of progress for a long time. That they blew ill now came as no real surprise. Still, he thought he might bargain. But before he could open his mouth to speak, he saw in Jakob's face that there would be no friendly negotiation. In Jakob Miller's tight, close world, Jess was a fellow human—but of another species. Mostly, he was not Amish.

Within minutes of leaving the factory, Jess had also left behind the spare Amish countryside—stark whitewashed houses with single-curtained windows set alongside neat, spreading fields—and was back in Butler County, where the farms were hidden away behind the trees and hills and had to be stumbled on like duck's nests. He found himself pondering the laws of human kinship. They were laws nowhere recorded, as far as Jess knew, but binding just the same. A brother by blood might be always a stranger. And though you shared no family ties, a friend like Pat Badger could become your next of kin, someone you could trust with your life. But there would always be those, like Jakob, who were destined, were decreed, to remain a mere acquaintance.

10

DAVID SLEPT FITFULLY, his eyelids twitching. Tsura turned away and gazed out the hospital window. She wondered if the other buildings she could see along the street were as cold inside as this one. A steady, frigid wind blew from a slotted opening in the ceiling. The unnatural temperature made her uneasy when it was so warm outside. She moved her chair a little closer to the bed, so as not to feel the blast directly. At the sound of her rustling, David opened his eyes. They were glazed and dark with pain. They fixed themselves to hers.

"Tsura."

"Yah," she said. "I'm here."

"We didn't make it to the gorge."

"Yah. We didn't make it to the gorge."

"What happened?"

"You don't remember?"

"Nope."

"Nothing?"

"I remember we were going to the mill. And I remember the possum. After that, it all goes black."

"Yah. When you swerved for the possum, we got off the road pretty bad. Over the cliff and into a tree. Good strong tree, though. It stopped us falling all the way down."

"Good tree," David agreed. "You weren't hurt?"

"Not a little bit."

"Good tree," David said again, and closed his eyes.

The doctor had put something into his arm with a needle to help with the pain. It seemed also to make him sleep. Tsura was glad. The longer he slept, the longer it would be until he learned that the bones in his legs were broken in such a way that he might never walk again, and if he did, it would not be with ease. Although there was nothing more she wanted to see from it, she turned back to the window and gazed out. There was a smell of death in this place, underneath all the other odors. David was alive, at least. And he would not go to war.

Tsura could not help thinking of Eli then, passing alone on a hilltop into that world he had spent so many morbid hours fearing. Why he was so haunted she would never know. But she was glad he was free of the curse. How she longed sometimes, though, to see his gray eyes clear and shining as he showed her some new trick he had taught Bell to do, or to hear him say roughly, "Girl, your pies is getting better. Though you still do not bake so good as my mother." Eli had really missed his family. So much so that when he was in a spell he would call her Ruth, his favorite sister's name. He talked little about it, but she did know that he had not gone away on his own. He had been sent.

"Amish law," Eli said. "A man must submit, must bend his will, or be put out." She knew, though, that he could not repent the things he did that his people found so upsetting, could not dam the thoughts and plans that rushed into his head unbidden at times and left him so disordered. Amish life was order. Without repentance, Eli had said, when she protested, there could be no forgiveness. No possibility of a reunion. This was also the Amish way. Tsura was secretly glad she had not been born Amish and so was unbound to keep their laws. In their stead, she had been pleased to grant Eli a full pardon.

He did not say it, but Tsura understood that his people had put him out only because they had not known what else to do. And it was being sent away from their own that had brought Eli and her mother together. A husbandless gypsy girl, heavy with child, sheltered on a rain-soaked night in the house of a mad Amish man. "A pair of mountain castaways," Pat Badger always called them, when telling Tsura the story of her birth. "A most peculiar alliance."

The door to David's hospital room suddenly swung open, and a nurse entered, bringing with her a smell of rubbing alcohol and cigarette smoke.

"I need to check vitals," she said briskly, taking David's wrist in her hand. He stirred but did not open his eyes. While the nurse stared at her watch, she took deep breaths and let them out slowly, like a sigh. She had a permanently weary look. The deep creases at the corners of her mouth turned down, and there were dark half-moon shadows under her eyes. Her fingernails were yellow. She wrote something on the chart at the end of the bed. She lifted the bag of fluid hanging on the metal rack, examined it, and wrote on her chart again. When she was done, she looked over at Tsura.

"You must be family," she said with a quick, sly wink. Tsura understood the woman was saying one thing and meaning something else. What it was she did mean Tsura did not know, and did not wish explained. She looked at the floor and kept silent.

A few minutes after the nurse had gone, Lester arrived with Margit Busco. "My Got, he's unconscious," Margit said, shuffling over as quickly as her old stiff hips would let her to David's side.

"You heard the nurse, Anya," Lester said. "They've sedated him. It's not so bad as it looks, I'm sure."

"Two smashed kneecaps? A snapped femur? A crushed pelvis? How you can say it's not so bad? I don't like that nurse, Lester. Her uniform is dirty, and she smokes. I smell it. You gonna go ask the doctor to get some better nurse for our Davit."

"One old chimney sniffs out another," Lester grinned, shaking his head. Margit Busco didn't smile. She looked frightened. Lester put his arm around his tiny grandmother. He stroked her back, rubbing the hump where her spine bowed out. "Anya," he said gently. "She's done a good job. Look at him. He thinks he's passed out under that big sycamore, down by the creek. Anyway, if I asked for a better nurse, they'd send a worse one. I promise."

Margit still clutched Lester's arm, but she seemed soothed.

Tsura listened. Her heart ached to hear their familial talk. She felt keenly alone. Quietly, without being seen, she rose and left the room.

Jess stood at the kitchen window, watching the headlights pass as Margit and Lester left again for the hospital. There was just no way, he'd decided, to be ready for what life would bring. You could tune to the rhythm of the seasons, live by the almanac, plant and harvest crops with the blessing of the moon. You could make plans and figure on the outcome, increasing your stock by methods handed across generations. All with an optimism born of experience. But for all your careful plotting toward every eventuality, all your scanning the horizon and keeping your hand to the plow, there would come an instant when the planet would jerk to a sudden halt. Nothing you could do but stand still and wait.

Gracie had thought hardship was allowed by God as a kind of training for the soul. Suffering was not only a natural part of life, a thing to be endured until it passed, as animals do. It could transform. You could emerge from its darkness with more light than you had. Be better than you were. Become a saint. It was this belief of hers that used to secretly comfort Jess, because it allowed him to yield his anxiousness to her certainty. "It will be all right," she would say in a tone that caused Jess to believe that it would. Even when he knew for sure that it couldn't. He could hear her saying it now, for incredibly—though the reality of Gracie was fading, and some days he worked hard to recall the scent of her hair or the warm, gold glow of her eyes—his impression of her was strong, her voice in his head as calm and reassuring as it had ever been, perhaps more.

He was surprised to find himself considering that she may have had it right about suffering. He had never wanted to believe it could have meaning, but what if it did? What if it could transform darkness into light? One thing was sure, it was the lot of humans to suffer. And his father's way, the way of stark reality—"This is all there is, son. Look for more and you'll miss it"—had left the wrong taste in his mouth. There was no sweetness in it. It was salt when he craved honey. It had served him all right, for a time, had perhaps even kept him alive, but it wasn't enough now. He needed more.

The percolator sputtered and fell quiet. Jess went to the cupboard and took down a cup. Looking across the way, he saw a soft, unsteady glow at the Busco house, a flickering he guessed to be candlelight. Margit's sister-in-law, Nora, would be praying. On the wall of the Busco kitchen, he knew, there hung a flowery-bordered picture of a swarthy, Hungarian Jesus holding his own heart, red and glowing, in the palm of his hand. As a boy, Jess had found the image disturbing. Irresistibly so. He had in fact worked awfully hard to peel his gaze away from it. He could not fathom what sort of comfort such an image might have to offer. After a time, though, he learned that the picture was sacred to the family, brought from the old country by Margit's father, and that in difficult hours a candle would be lit in front of it to burn day and night for as long as the trouble lasted, much as oil lamps now burned before the faces of saints in almost every room of Jess's own home. He had sometimes thought Gracie too fervent in her religion, all the repenting and rejoicing, so many feasts and fasts. Her piety was mild next to Darya's.

Nellie whined at the back door, and Jess left the window to go over and let her in. She breezed past him, trolled along the baseboards for remnants of last night's meal, found a good-sized chunk of bread that would never have been there in Gracie's day, and then lay down with it cradled between her paws, her tail thumping a victory tune against the floor. He looked again at the flickering light across the way and thought of the Busco women and all the times over their many years they would have had need to light that candle, thought of all the times he might have lit one too, had he been the candle-lighting kind. He found himself going into the living room, then, and standing before the icons.

The lampada was cold and dark. Darya had been busy with the baby, had just gone back to bed after the four-o'clock feeding. Jess didn't attempt to light it. Instead, he rummaged in the drawer and found a taper and a match. He set the taper in the little brass candle-stand and lit it. When the wick had caught, and the flame was burning bright, he stood for a long moment, gazing into the eyes of Christ. His heart was full. Wordlessly, he poured out his ache for Gracie, confessed that he could not hold their child in his arms for fear that if he loved her, she too would be taken away. Released, as well, his burden over Tsura, his need to find her and ask her to come home. Finally, he requested a measure of mercy for David. Was any of this prayer? Jess didn't know. He hoped it was.

11

THE NEXT AFTERNOON Jess stopped by Rose Marie's house to return a dish, one of many he had been bringing back since the days of the funeral. Food was love to Rose Marie. Of course, her big warm family was still whole. She did not understand yet, and Jess hoped she would have no need to, not for a long time, how loss filled your whole being, even your belly. Jess himself had grown very lean, almost skeletal, as if because he and Gracie were one flesh his had naturally gone with her to the grave. In fact, the only person at the farm with any appetite at all right now was an infant. Rose Marie did not know it, but her lasagnas had more than once been slipped next door for the Busco boys to consume.

Rose Marie looked tired. Aside from missing Gracie, Jess knew she had worries of her own. Her husband's chronic unfaithfulness had at last been presented to her in such a way that she couldn't overlook it. Skip had fallen in love.

Jess did not stay long. But over a quick cup of coffee in her quiet kitchen (it being a school day), he mentioned that he was looking for Tsura, that he had thought to traipse the woods along Muddy Creek that afternoon before evening chores to see if he could find her.

"You make it sound as if she's lost," Rose Marie said with a wan, dry smile when he had finished. "From just the little I know of Tsura, it wouldn't surprise me to find out she's staying away for reasons of her own." She smiled, gave Jess a gentler, more sympathetic look. "She's an odd one, that girl. Have you considered that this may have nothing to do with you?"

Jess had, in fact, not considered it. And it gave him a great deal to think about on the drive home. Not once in all his fretting had it crossed his mind to wonder if Tsura might have a reason other than his ill-treatment of her for retreating, the way she had, to the woods. "It happens, you know," Rose Marie had finished flatly, "that we sometimes overestimate our own importance." And though Jess suspected she was talking to herself as much as to him, he had to consider that where he was concerned, she had touched on a truth.

Considering the matter, it seemed to Jess that he was being humbled on purpose, as if having stood for a few brief moments before the icon of Christ, he was now somehow standing within it, viewing himself through those all-seeing eyes. And from this view it was pretty clear that he had acquired more than just his father's so-called natural way of taking his place the world. He had also acquired his stiff-neckedness. "There's a way seems right to man," he remembered Orville Hays saying, "and oft times it isn't." Jess wondered then if this was to be the response to his prayer. (If indeed such silent groaning was prayer.) God, after all these years, speaking to him in voices he could recognize. Or (and this was a sorrowful thought, weighted with regret) it could be that God had been speaking all along, and Jess only could not hear because he was not with any real amount of honesty listening. To be sure, there had been a great deal of motioning toward it, of cupping his hand to his ear and craning his neck heavenward. But he had begun to suspect himself now, and pretty strongly, of also plugging the sound hole with his thumb. For as Millie used to say, once you knew, you had to do.

Tsura woke to the ringing of the monastery bells. She rose and gathered together her small belongings, putting into the cotton drawstring bag—along with the two hardboiled eggs and rye and onion sandwich it still held—a box of matches and the toiletry set Gracie had given her and taught her to use. She folded her bedroll into a neat bundle, setting it on the limestone ledge where she had slept. Outside she went to the place in the rocky, moss-coated hillside where water trickled out in a thin, cold stream from some high hidden source. She cupped her hands and drank deeply, then cleaned her teeth and washed her face and ran a comb over her curls.

She was disturbed in her spirit. To the east, she felt the firm, gentle pull of the monastery. From the west came an unsettling hum, like the gathering of wasps, about which she had received no knowledge or instruction, but which seemed to be drawing her just the same. For the first time in her life she was unsure which direction to take. After a moment, she had decided. She would go west.

12

THE FELLOW HARLAN had hired for warehouse help had a low, snide way. Working with him, Jess wanted all the time to feel his back pocket and make sure his wallet was still there. Ace was one of those types, too, who had a way of being busy when the boss was around, always lazing when he wasn't, forever jagging around or asking fresh, forward questions that bent your nerves and left you feeling jittery. Just all around the sort of man you couldn't trust or like. Jess was not pleased, his first day back at the feed store, to be stuck in the warehouse with him. But there were no deliveries to make, and since Harlan was the boss, he had no choice. At the moment, Ace was on Jess's side of the pallet of grass seed they were supposed be unloading, crowding him into the wall.

"What'ya say we take a break?" Ace said. "I need a smoke."

"You just smoked two of those things less than an hour ago," Jess said irritably, and moved to the other side of the pallet. "What do you say you give your lungs a rest, and help me finish moving this seed?"

"'Cuz you're makin' it look like a one-man job, that's why."

Ace ambled over to the open door and seated himself on a low stack of salt blocks. He leaned back against the wall, pulled a cigarette from his pocket, and tapped it against his palm. As he put it to his lips, he was deliberately nonchalant, lit it slowly, drew hard, and exhaled a thin stream of smoke, regarding Jess with a sly expression. He left the cigarette dangling from his lip and stretched his legs out straight. He waggled his feet.

"Jess," he said, examining his legs, "did you ever hear of a phantom limb?"

"Yep."

"Well, I know a guy, wasn't three days in Vietnam when he got his leg blown off stepping on a land mine. Came home draggin' a stump, swore he still had feeling in it. Said he was all the time gettin' a sharp, stabbing pain in his foot. He claimed he could wiggle his toes. You believe that?"

"I don't know of a reason why I shouldn't."

"Well, I say he's full of horseshit. Ain't no way a fellow's gonna feel something in a foot that ain't there. Just ain't no way." He looked over at Jess, head cocked at a skeptical angle. "What do you think, that all them teeny-tiny pieces he left back there in the jungle are feeling him at the same time?"

"I don't know," Jess said. "Maybe they are."

"Naw. They ain't. And he ain't wiggling his toes, neither. I'd bet this pack of Marlboros on it."

"You'd be wasting your wager on me," Jess said. "I don't gamble. And I don't smoke."

"No kiddin'? I never would have took you for a holy roller."

"I'm not."

"Say, Jess. Harlan just told me this morning about your wife. I'm real sorry to hear it."

"Thanks," Jess said shortly. There had been no sincerity in the man's tone. He wasn't about to waste any replying.

"I never had the pleasure to meet her," Ace added, looking slighted. He was silent for a moment, examining his cigarette. Then he said, "Was she pretty?"

Jess grabbed an end-roll of chicken wire and threw it over in the corner, out of the way.

"Yep."

"Pretty as that little Italian woman I see you talking to all the time over at the deli?"

"I don't know. I can't remember ever comparing my wife to Rose Marie Patterson."

Ace paused in his smoking to try out the name. "Rose Marie."

He scraped the palms of his hands with his fingernails, then scratched them hard, as if he had got a sudden itch, and stared out the door.

Jess threw the last bag of seed to the top of the stack and moved over a few feet, to a pallet of oats.

Ace took another drag from his cigarette.

"From what I can tell, Jess," he said, opening his mouth wide to show his tongue, flicking it in a lewd way as he exhaled, "you and that Rose Marie seem like good friends."

Jess felt suddenly queasy.

Ace grinned, an obscene splitting of his lower face. He threw the butt of his cigarette down and crushed it with the heel of his boot, stepped in so close Jess caught the faint, foul smell of a tooth going bad, felt the hot humid rush of the man's breath in his ear, the ugly hiss of Ace's suggestion, whispered so low Jess could barely hear it.

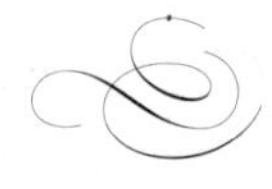

He sat in his big easy chair that evening, nursing his right hand with an ice pack. His fist hadn't hurt when it was balling up to crack Ace's jaw. It ached like the dickens now, but he couldn't feel a thing then. Or hear anything, either, for that matter. He was so far gone by the time he'd hit the man, Harlan had to tell him three times it was over. Ace Vanzandt was out cold. Go home.

"I said go home, Jesse."

The light from the lamp drew a circle around Nellie, lying on the floor at his feet. His *Journals* lay unread across his knees. Out in the kitchen, Darya had the baby in the sink. She was singing a soft, lilting song as she washed, splashing water in a steady rhythm. Every so often the singing stopped. Then, after a second or two of silence, it would begin again. Jess did not need to see to know that the bathwater would be mingled with tears. He set down the *Journals*, gingerly, careful of his hand, and taking the ice pack with him, went out to stand on the porch. The air was colder than it had been in a while. Wherever Tsura was tonight, he hoped she was keeping warm.

He turned toward the east and saw the glow of firelight in the lower field. The travelers had arrived. Suddenly the blank, black space in his memory cleared, a leering face loomed, and he remembered something Ace had said earlier in the day, before Jess had set his jaw sideways.

"You know, everybody's sayin' them travelin' girls are the friendly type. I'm thinking to ease out that way tonight and see if I can't make myself acquainted."

All his intention to leave Tsura to her forest hermitage flew away in that instant. He threw down the ice pack and thrust his hand into his pocket, ignoring the pain. Truck keys in hand, he stepped off the porch. Ace Vanzandt was the sort of man you could knock into kingdom come and within the hour he'd have found his way back to trouble. Wrong or right, Jess was going to find Tsura.

13

HE DROVE THREE MILES down the road, parked on the shoulder, and began his search in the woods that stood on his side of the property line between the farm and what was now monastery land, the Hays's old place. These woods stood in sassafras, oak, hickory, and the massive old sycamores that guarded Muddy Creek. The woods were bosky here, and he set a slow pace, combing ground dense with vine cover, watching closely for signs of recent change: raw ends of freshly broken twigs, newly turned leaves or, if he was very lucky, footprints pressed into the soft soil.

Jess knew a little about tracking. His father had often taken him on long searches like this one through the woods when he was a youngster, following the trail of local deer herds and the men that hunted them. Clyde had no Indian blood—a great-grandmother on their mother's side had first owned Walter's black walnut eyes and Jess's hair. But despite this lack, a primitive instinct seemed somehow to rise in Clyde whenever he entered the woods. Jess had always thrilled to the sight of his father's long nostrils flaring to catch a scent on the breeze or his flinty gaze narrowing as he spotted a set of twin depressions near the base of a tree that meant a man had cooled his heels there.

Jess stopped suddenly in his tracking and listened, his ear sifting through the forest noise. He had thought he detected a human sound. A rustle of clothing. He stood motionless. After a minute, though, he decided there was nothing out of the ordinary to hear. With his gaze, he sectioned off another square section, keeping it to about twenty-five feet, as his father had taught him to do, and began to scan the ground again in the pieced, patchy light still slanting through the tree canopy.

Clyde hated a trespasser. Especially a sport-hunting trespasser. There was little that could raise his ire like having men on his land with guns and no prior permission. He didn't always catch them. Jess recalled vividly sitting up in the darkness as a child, having been awakened by the crack of his father's old double-barreled shotgun firing into the air. More than once he had crept out of bed and peered down from the window in the upstairs hall to see his father, clad only in his underwear, standing in the light of the porch and shouting into the darkness at some poor city hunter who'd missed the sign out on the road.

The light was fading fast. It was full dark already in the trees. Jess had seen no sign of Tsura or her camp, which did not surprise him much. Darya's directions were the sort given by people who could send you to a specific Kosher meat shop on Squirrel Hill in Pittsburgh, not the kind you needed to find a girl in these hills who was *of* the forest, and not only living in it. Reluctantly, he decided to go back to his truck and drive down to the sled path that ran alongside his own east field. He could park there and walk across the field to the place where he had seen the light of the campfire beginning to burn bright. Before it got too late, he should have a talk with the travelers.

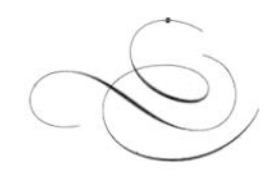

Ace Vanzandt drove slow around a curve, rubbing his jaw. There was something off, he had decided, with Jess Hazel. Way off. Having his wife die the way she did, so sudden and all, must've rattled a screw loose in his head. Flat out, hell-damned crazy, that's what the man was. Had them long arms too. Like a baboon. You had to watch those stringy, quiet types. Ace knew that. He'd just got plumb careless and forgot.

There was a little something that would soothe, though, if he could just find it. He drove around another curve, searching for firelight, the shadows of people moving about a field, anything besides the lonesome piece of road he could see by a single beam of headlight. The other one was out. Something was always out on this car because the boss had sold him a lemon. A big, black, gas-eating Buick lemon. Which was just like Harlan Christie. And Ace had got duped by the guys at the bar too. There was nothing going on out here. Nothing at all.

"Wait, now," he said suddenly, slowing the car to a crawl. "Look there, Ace. At the edge of them woods." That was something.

He leaned across the seat and rolled the passenger-side window down, peering out into the darkness. There it was again.

A white flash of skirt.

He could see her now, had a full view of her silhouette. Damn. She was a girl, all right. His hands tingled, a familiar sensation.

"That, my friend," he said, talking to himself in a sing-song voice, "ain't nothin." He scraped his fingernails down his palms, scratching the itch.

He switched off the headlights, crept along in the dark to where the woods began, pulled over, and parked. He slid silently out of the car and swung the door closed, careful not to let it make a sound as it latched. Anticipation spread warm through his core as he moved in her direction. He sucked air through his teeth, quickening his pace. It was lucky there was no fence to have to go slithering under on his belly, slowing him down and grinding dirt into his best pair of blue jeans. The field was wide, plowed in dark furrows. He shivered, didn't care for the eerie feeling it gave him, stretched out there in the darkness. Didn't care for it at all. It made him think too much of being a child, left to sit alone on the beach at night while his mother went off to play in the grass with a man. "Be a good boy, now," she'd say, "no following," with that high girly giggle that was so not like her real laugh. Not her deep, sweet chuckle.

He never followed, either. No matter how scared he got. The dark water breathing in and out like something alive. The tide rising, pulling at his feet, eating away at the sand.

"Well, no more," he murmured softly. "Ace is not a good boy now, Mama. Not a good boy at all."

He broke into a kind of squatting trot, bending his knees and keeping low as he ran along the uncut edge of the field. No need to startle her. Not that he minded a good chase, but she was tall and had legs like a deer. Might be too swift to catch. Anyway, he'd almost reached her. She was close enough now to touch.

Man. This was a gift, that's what it was. A pure, sweet, beautiful gift left out here under the stars for wicked, bad old Ace Vanzandt to unwrap. And all alone too. No one coming from behind, out of the field. No one going into the woods with her.

Only him.

14

TSURA WAS WALKING as the crow would fly, from woods to field to woods again. She had gone about four miles when she reached the stand of trees that marked the eastern edge of Hazel Valley. The buzzing had grown louder but more concentrated, as if the wasps had found a place to swarm. She had spent the day digging root plants along the banks of Muddy Creek, and although she now had a good offering of sassafras, burdock, and dandelion in her bag to take as a gift to Darya, she thought that she should not have lingered so long. Night had fallen quick and dense, the way it did in autumn, and she was forced to sweep the horizon with her gaze to see what obstacles might lie in her path in the darkness. It was cold. Colder than it had been on previous nights. She blew on her hands, rubbing them together. The bedroll was still in the cave, or she might have stopped to wrap herself in it before pressing on. As she neared the old sled path that led to the apple orchard, she saw that there was firelight in Jess's east field. She drew nearer still and saw a truck parked in the sled path, and heading westward from it, the long lean figure of a man, making his way across the field toward the fire. Her heart caught. Eli had walked that way, shoulders bowed, head down, as if he had lost something important and would spend the rest of his life looking for it.

The buzzing had grown very loud, but her spirit was quiet now, detached from the din. No image flashed, no instruction came. Not in the old way. But still she saw. The knowledge was bittersweet, but she saw now why, despite the call of the monastery, she had chosen this direction to come.

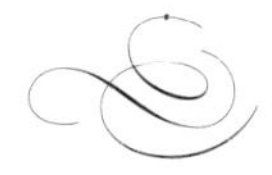

Back at home, the house asleep and quiet, Jess sat in the lamplight again, his *Journals* open on his knees, gazing at a single line on the page. For a long time, he had been staring at the words without seeing them, but now this one sentence stood out, bold and clear.

And we proceeded on.

He smiled a little, with Tsura asleep upstairs in her old room, to think how foolish he had been, believing he was going to save her. There she was, coming alongside him out of nowhere in the dark. Walking in silence with him to the spot where the travelers were camped, then back again to the truck, and home, as if there had never been any trouble between them. All was forgiven. Of her own will, she had come home. And now the Hazel family, what was left of it, would proceed on.

The travelers had invited them to sit awhile by the fire, and Jess had surprised himself, and probably Tsura, by saying, "All right." A pipe was being passed around, and a boy with long lank hair and a many-colored coat like Joseph's offered it to Jess. "Peace pipe," the boy said, as if he needed explain. Not wishing to be unpeaceful, Jess took it. The smoke rising from the bowl was like that of the wild grapevine he and Walter used to smoke in the woods as boys. Jess had never much liked inhaling it, not as Walter did. Nor had he been very good at it. He set the pipe briefly between his teeth, then passed it on. Once it had gone around the circle a few times and the smell of woodsmoke was mixed with the acrid odor of the stuff in the pipe, the travelers began to talk of the gathering they had been to and of the wondrous things that had taken place. They talked of possibilities, of progress, of a dream that was growing into reality. Spoke of an Earth restored, someday, to such beauty by their efforts, it would come to take the place of heaven in the minds of the enlightened. Mostly though, they talked of themselves. Over and over, though they were none of them anywhere near so young as Tsura, the travelers referred to themselves as children. Jess did not mock, but watching Tsura there at the fire, old and wise as the mountain of her birth and yet younger than any of them, he felt they could not have found a word more fitting.

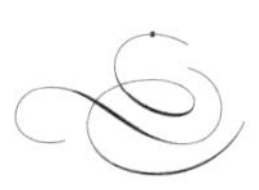

When Tsura and Jess had taken their leave of the group and had got into the truck together, Jess turned to her, acutely aware that he would be speaking the first words he had said to her since the night of Gracie's death. He poured all the depth of his feeling into small, plain words.

"Are you all right?"

"Yah. Fine."

"I'm so glad," Jess said, his throat tight with emotion. He waited then to see if she would say more. There was so much in his heart, but it was Tsura who had found him, not the other way around. Sensing that she knew all anyway, he waited, silent and hopeful. Reconciliation, if there was to be any, was in her hands. Her next words stunned him. She spoke as if nothing had passed between them at all.

"Yah. I was just thinking that them people back there talk the same as nuns. Peace. Love. Brother. Sister. But this is different," she tapped her chest.

"This?"

"The light."

Jess looked at her, still more surprised. The truck cab was dark, but it seemed as if he were staring into the face in the icon all over again, feeling the same sweet fear. Those eyes. They saw so much.

"Do you often see light in people?" he asked. "I mean, other than nuns?"

She turned to look at him. "Yah. Sure. You got it," she said simply. "Not like the nuns, though. I guess they got them prayers. Yours is small. Flickery. Like a lit match."

"Well," Jess said, at a loss, and they drove the rest of the way up the hill to the house in silence.

When Jess got to work the next day, Harlan came out of the office.

"Ace won't be coming in," he said. "Not for a good while. Several weeks, at least. And don't think it's because you made his left ear sit crooked. If that was it, I'd be docking your pay."

"Is he sick?" Jess asked, working hard at not looking pleased.

"Not exactly. It's kind of a crazy thing, to tell you the truth. He evidently stumbled into the hospital at Ellwood City last night yelling at the top of his lungs about how he'd all of a sudden gone blind, had to get some good samaritan to get him to the Emergency. I guess he wasn't lying, either. The nurse who called said his corneas had a sort of whitish-blue film over them. He really couldn't see a thing. It'll take a specialist, I guess, to know for sure, but the doctor there thinks it may be temporary. Anyway, the nurse said he was raving when he came in, had some crazy, wild story to tell about what happened, but not a bit of what he said made any sense."

That sounded to Jess like Ace Vanzandt.

"What did he say happened?

Harlan laughed.

"Well, now, there's the crazy part. He claimed all he did was grab a pretty girl by the waist."

15

CHRISTMAS CAME and went unremarked. It was only when he saw the wreaths still up on Main Street in Rose Point after New Year's, and he thought of the one Gracie had always made for Becky's stall door, that Jess realized he had missed it. Russian Christmas on the seventh of January was less festive than usual too, though not at all forgotten. Ivan and Darya left the baby with Tsura and went to the midnight Nativity Vigil at the Russian Orthodox church in New Castle. The drive was worth it, Ivan said, because Father Antony tended to pray more in English than Darya cared to hear on Christmas night, when she was always homesick. Jess milked alone next morning because Ivan slept in. After a breakfast prepared so late in the day it was almost dinner, the old man dozed again in Jess's chair while Darya crept upstairs with small furtive gifts for Tsura and a garish, grinning stuffed monkey to put in the baby's crib.

Jess was blue for days.

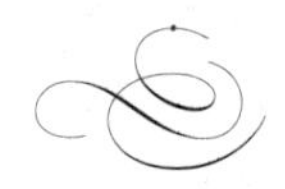

Later in the month, toward the end, it snowed eleven inches. A clean, thick white blanket of down that in the night quietly settled itself over the old snow, grown dingy and tired. Jess rose to a world refreshed. Seeing the farm looking so brightened, so hopeful, he felt a flicker of hope in his own chest, a spark of the wonder he'd felt on such a morning as a child. Even the cows seemed cheered, almost charmed. They still stood knee deep in it when he and Ivan reached the milking shed, the entire herd so quiet and content, though their bags were full and dragging the snow, that Jess finally had to ask the boss cow to bring them in. He went about his work with a lighter step, his back straighter and his shoulders lifted, like a horse whose load has been ever so slightly lessened. Only when he left the barn and went up the hill to the house did his mood fall. Sitting down to breakfast, Jess saw that Tsura's chair at the table was empty. Not to worry, Darya said, Tsura would be back before lunch. But when Jess asked where it was she had gone, Darya suddenly forgot her English. She lapsed into Russian, trying to explain. Suspecting strongly that he was being deceived anyway, Jess did not stay to listen. He laid his napkin next to his plate and rose from his chair, no longer hungry.

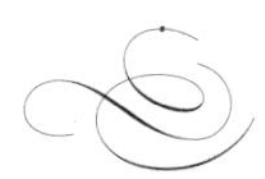

On Groundhog Day, Rose Marie called Jess at the feed store to ask if he would come by her house when he got off work. And hearing a worrisome dullness in her voice, Jess quickly agreed.

"Skip got his divorce," she said flatly before hanging up. "I got served this morning at 9:05. It's not even noon yet, and he's already moved out. Gone. Like he never lived here. Like I had all these kids on my own."

"Lord, Rose Marie," Jess said quietly. "What will you do?"

"I'm going to sell this place and move in with the folks," she said. "And I need your help."

"Sure. Of course. What sort of help?"

"Your shoulder, mostly. And a ladder, so I can cry on it."

Jess was not all that surprised at Rose Marie's news, more so to hear the shock she'd received in her voice. It must be one thing, he decided, while driving over to her house after work, for a woman to know she has never been precious to her husband, that though they've been married twelve years, there was never a time when he held her love in awe or found her trust in him sacred enough not to break. Another thing altogether to have the proof of his lack served up to her on a plate in writing.

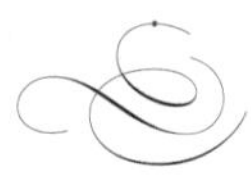

"Are you sure about this?" Jess said, looking around Rose Marie's rambling old four-bedroom house, once he was there. "There can't be more than nine hundred square feet of living space in your folks' apartment. You'll be stacked in like cordwood."

"Don't forget I grew up in that apartment," she said. "We managed it all right. And I don't see how I have a choice," she said, flatly giving a shrug. "Skip has turned out to be quite a bit more than a cheat. He's a con artist. I don't know what he had to pay that fancy Pittsburgh lawyer, but whatever it was, the man made it well worth his while. The pittance I'll be getting each month isn't enough to feed a canary, much less five children."

Jess did not know what to say to that. He was worried for her, though, losing her husband and now her home, having to move into a flat no bigger than a cigar box with her parents. A whole life lost in a fell swoop. It was a kind of sudden death. There would be grief in it, he realized, and the thought pained him. He wished for a solution. A memory struck him then, a conversation he and Gracie had once had. She had just come home from church and was fussing about the kitchen as she always did, getting Jess's noon meal and making tea for herself.

"Jess," she had said, sitting down at the table with her cup, watching him go at the plate of eggs, wolfing down fried potatoes and bacon, "how far would you go to help a friend?" Church often provoked soberness in her, made her thoughtful. Jess hadn't been in the mood right then for deep conversation. He had laughed, he remembered.

"What, am I going to need a train ticket?"

"No," she'd said, still serious. "At least, I don't think so. I was just thinking of the sick man in the Gospel. The one whose friends let him down with ropes through a hole they made in the roof of a house." She sipped her tea, her eyes on his face. "I'm just wondering. Would we trouble ourselves that much for someone?"

Jess had laughed at her, again saying "we." Gracie's heart was a five-star hotel, had a smiling porter out front waving folks inside. His was the one-room shack.

But what if right now, here in front of him, was the chance to remodel? Add on. Expand.

"Hey, Rose Marie," he said slowly. She had just put a slice of panettone on a plate for him, had the coffee pot in one hand, and was reaching for a cup with the other. "Why don't you and the kids move out to the farm. Live with me?"

Rose Marie set down the coffee pot slowly, as if she feared dropping it. She turned from the counter to face Jess, her brown eyes wide with shock.

"I'm dead serious. Even with the Morozovs and Tsura, there's room."

"You forgot the baby."

"And the baby."

"No," she said firmly, shaking her head. "It would be the same as shacking up, in the eyes of this town. The deli customers would make my folks miserable over it. They'd never live it down."

He was relieved to hear her say it. For it was pure craziness, of course. Trouble was, it seemed that now a stranger had taken charge of his jaw and was opening it again to speak. A man who had by nature more kindness, more compassion, more courage than Jess.

"Then let's get married," he said.

"My God, Jess!" she said. "Now you're just absurd." She appeared to consider it, though, crossed her arms and gazed off, looking out the window. And when she turned her eyes to his again, there was a look in them Jess had never seen. They were suddenly velveted, dark and warm. He stood stock still, floored. And then, unexpectedly, stirred. But she said, quickly, "No." And though her voice was soft, even trembling a little, her meaning was firm. She turned away then, opened a drawer, and took out a spoon. When she swung around again, the look was gone. She had tears in her eyes. Waving her hand for Jess to sit, she set out the sugar bowl and the spoon, filled the cups with coffee.

Jess took a chair, his legs grateful to be sitting.

"Let's talk about you," she said, blotting at her eyes with the cuff of her blouse. She spoke now in her old, sisterly way. "How are things with Tsura? Are you two getting along?"

"Oh, sure. We get along fine," Jess said.

"Really? Because fine is not what I hear in your voice."

"Well, we do," he insisted.

She frowned.

"It's only that—well, I guess I thought she'd be happier, being handed a family. Her heart's just not in it. Not with us."

"Where is it, do you think?"

"I'm not qualified to say." Jess felt himself sinking. "All I know is," he said dully, "it seems to be in the woods. She goes there often enough."

Rose Marie looked at him, eyebrows raised in surprise.

"It's not the woods she goes to, Jess," she said gently. "I thought you knew that. It's the convent. The nuns."

Jess sat up straight.

"What nuns?" he said. "Gracie's nuns? How do you know?"

"David Busco. He's been bringing Mama fish on Fridays."

Jess set his cup down. He pushed his chair away from the table and set his hands on his knees. A sudden dispirited, helpless feeling seeped into his chest, as if a storm had begun to blow and things he thought he'd buttoned down fast were loose and flapping in the wind.

"Why," he said slowly, "if Tsura's keen on seeing nuns, all she needs is to ask. I'd drive her out to Mill Bend anytime she wants, in the truck."

Rose Marie's eyes shifted to the wall opposite the sink, where there was a bare spot in need of paint. For a long silent moment, she peered intently at it.

Jess shifted in his chair uneasy. "Seems like you don't believe me."

She didn't answer, only rose quietly and fetched the coffee pot from the stove, poured them both another cup. They sat in uncomfortable silence for a while then, drinking. As they sat, Jess tried to imagine Tsura, in whom it seemed there was no guile, sneaking off in secret to see the nuns.

"Hey," Rose Marie said suddenly, in a false, bright tone designed to end the silence, "did you hear there's a hippie couple squatting in Zook's house, up on Kerry Mountain?"

"No," he said absently. "I didn't hear."

"There is," Rose Marie said. "Mama said they came into the deli the other day, asking to sample the cheese. She said they acted like it was as natural as rain, a white boy and a colored girl, walking around in her store, holding hands."

"Well," Jess said, and trailed off, considering now the watchfulness in a certain set of coal-black eyes. Watching. Watching. Always watching. And waiting. Waiting for what? A blessing from him to go the monastery? He wasn't a priest. Hell, he wasn't even a father.

Rose Marie laughed. "You didn't hear all right. Not a word I've said."

"I did too. A hippie couple in the deli, buying cheese."

"Sampling cheese," she said dryly. "And holding hands."

16

WINTER GREW BITTER as it wore on. It was harsher than any in Jess's recent memory and tested him sore.

At the beginning of February, Jakob Miller stopped buying Hazel Valley milk completely, and Jess was forced to take full-time shifts at the Feed & Seed. In March the time for Lent came and the Morozovs began to fast. Ivan's eyes, which had begun to show a certain jolly glint, especially in the company of Tsura, became once more sad and pensive. Darya too, perhaps because she could not comfort Ivan with cabbage rolls or pirozhki, seemed distant, preoccupied, less the reassuring presence Jess had come to depend on her to be. Only Tsura and the baby, who had never eaten meat in any case, did not seem to suffer in the two long months of deprivation.

Tsura was the same as ever. She did not seem happy. But Jess could not call her sad. Watching her day after day, helping Darya care for the baby or willingly taking on chores around the house, he was ever more baffled, even vexed at times, by her behavior. She had wings but did not choose to fly.

In the last week of March, Father Antony finally baptized the baby, a thing Darya had been pressing for since at least October.

"What's the rush?" Jess had said obstinately when she first brought it up. "She's only been in the world a few weeks. When would she have found time to sin?"

Darya was a practical, and clever, woman. "The small baby is much easier to baptize than the big one," she said simply, to which Jess, having no experience with baptism other than his own, had no ready reply.

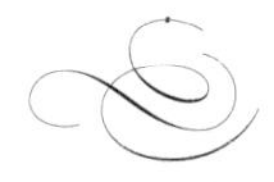

Only afterward, when Jess climbed the stairs to Tsura's room that Saturday evening of the baptism, did he learn what was in his heart. Only then did he know why he had resisted so long.

The baby was asleep in her crib. Jess crossed the room to look. A small nightlight glowed above the changing table. By its soft light, he could just make out the features that so often made him ache, the reasons he could not allow himself to gaze too closely at her. The unmistakable Russian roundness to the tip of her nose. The precious, Gracie-like curve where her ear joined her tiny jaw. She was illumined, according to Father Antony. "The child of God, Galina," he'd said, taking her three times under.

Illumined. Newly lit. *Like a match.*

She did have a certain glow, which Jess admitted could be the effect of the nightlight, for whether it was new or not, he could not say. There was something he could say, though, or he believed he could, here in this room, so tenderly lit. Her name. Gracie's name.

He laid his hand ever so gently on the small of the baby's back. She was warm, sweating. He spoke tentatively at first, whispering, trying it out, "Galina." And then he said it again, without hesitation, "Galina."

Suddenly she inhaled, drawing a long, quick breath in her sleep, as if startled in a dream. As she exhaled she sighed, shuddering, and Jess felt all the strength of her breath, her life, under his hand.

He began to shake.

And then, as if his shaking had at long last set his throat free, he began to weep. Undammed, the tears flowed in two continuous streams from his eyes, coursing down his face, soaking into the fabric of the baby's pajamas. They had been waiting a lifetime, those tears.

For the longest time he just stood there, weeping in the darkness, his hand on Galina's back.

He wept and wept.

17

BY THE TIME SPRING ARRIVED, it had become all too clear to Jess that Tsura would rather be at the monastery than at the farm. It was depressing, watching her stay when she didn't want to. This he said, with no small amount of bitterness, to Pat one cold, cloudless blue morning in April.

The dogwoods were in early first bloom, adorned like brides in petals of cleanest white. "The wise virgins," Gracie used to remark, every year when they flowered. They stood out so pure and virtuous, she said, awake and watchful, not like the oaks and hickories.

Jess and Pat were standing that morning out by the barnyard fence, watching Becky try out a new set of shoes. Tsura was a short distance away on the flat crest of the hill, in view but out of earshot, filling a basket with beets from the garden for Darya's soup.

"She's biding, Jesse."

"Biding?"

"Waiting."

"On what?'"

"You."

"Me? Why waiting on me? What have I got to do with it?"

Pat didn't answer. He looked at the ground, dug a crevice in the dirt with the toe of his boot. Jess flushed, felt the heat of anger creep over his neck. He'd seen that look before.

"You think she's here against her will."

"Not at all," Pat said mildly. "I'm saying it's Tsura's will that's keeping her here. She's gracing you. Loving you. Look, Jesse, you think she needs you. Needs family. But she doesn't. Not as you do. And if you've got some idea of penance, forget it. Any ill that was done came only to good. She's God's child. Born of the mountain dawn. She's not like the rest of us, you see, because she knows why she's alive. What she's for. She's always known, in her queer, wise way."

Jess was sorry now that he had spoken, for he knew already that he would not be pleased with the way this talk had gone when it was over and done.

"But everyone needs everyone else," he protested. "Isn't that what you always say? That together is the only way any of this works?"

"I do say that. And I believe it."

"You're not too keen on set-down religion, either, the way I remember it," Jess said. "You hate such rules and regulations."

"I do. But I'm not Tsura. For her kind, laws are only a different sort of freedom. Put her in jail and she'll sit there all right, but she'll be slipping through the bars at the same time, circling the valley on wings, high and free as a lark." Pat scuffed at the dirt again, shaking his head. "You think me so wise. She makes nonsense of me, that girl."

Jess would later have to agree, seeing that Pat had this time got it wrong.

Tsura was biding, all right. She was waiting on a word. But not from Jess.

18

In what seemed to Jess a mighty strange coincidence, he got a call from the abbess at the monastery that came only a day after his talk with Pat. Easter was just a few days away, she said, and the nuns wanted to make a kind of soft, quick cheese for baking sweets. Did the dairy have any extra milk to sell?

As he drove over late that afternoon with a ten-gallon milk can and two one-gallon cans of cream strapped behind the cab of his truck, Jess had no idea what he would see, not the slightest notion what a monastery looked like. He knew, because he had seen them from afar at the cemetery when they'd come for Gracie's burial, that the habits of these nuns were not the calf-length dress and simple kerchief Sister Vittoria had worn to teach at Mike and Rose Marie's school. The women at the funeral had been fully covered in long robes belted at the waist, had a kind of scarf draped over their heads, and a stiff, round hat. Everything was black. That was all he knew—and he admitted that it was not very much—of his wife's beloved nuns.

His first thought, as he drove through the arch-covered entrance, was that Zodie and Orville wouldn't know their old place. The house, fresh with warm brown paint, had been neatened up with flowers and a new brick walk to the porch. As Jess passed by it, a priest came out of the door, strode purposefully off the porch, and headed down the path, black robes swirling about his feet.

The main part of the monastery was set farther back from the entrance, away from the house, down a short but winding road. Perched on the last hill was a large chapel with a freestanding bell tower, surrounded by more neat flower beds that formed a cross-shaped courtyard. Across the courtyard stood a long, low building he decided must be the nuns' living quarters. He pulled into that drive and parked, got out, walked around to the truck bed, and began unstrapping the load of milk. There was a light wind, rustling the branches of the elms and oaks. And behind the chapel he could hear the creek rushing, hidden by a stand of thick woods. Below those sounds, though, there was a quiet to the place. A stillness that caused him to stop reaching for a milk can and just wait for a moment, taking it in.

"That is gift, you know," said a voice.

He turned and saw that the priest had made it to the top of the hill. The hill was steep, and when Jess had passed the man, he had been walking a quick pace, yet he was hardly out of breath. He could see now that the priest was older than he had appeared from a distance. But to match his youthful stride, he had an open expression, a boyish shine to his dark eyes. His beard was sparse, stiff, and grizzled. Jess realized then that he must have been staring, because the man smiled and said, "A gift, I said. To hear the quiet. Silence is a good teacher, but most of us make poor students."

Jess nodded mutely, suddenly sorry for his religious lack. There was a special greeting, he knew, for a priest, but he could not for the life of him remember what it was.

"You are a farmer," the priest said, nodding toward the truck.

"Yes, sir," Jess said, "I am. Hazel Valley Dairy. Just down the road."

"Ah. That explains it. A man of the earth. Your ear is trained. I came to here from Detroit. And before that, Bucaresti. A very noisy city. As all cities are, I suppose. Anyway, I had to learn to get used to this," he said, waving his hand. "It made me go a little crazy at first."

"I've never been to a city larger than Pittsburgh," Jess said, grinning. "I'll tell you, though, I only go there when I can't get out of it. And I'm always glad to get home."

A group of nuns came out of the long building then. They crossed the courtyard in silence and went into the chapel.

The priest suddenly gripped Jess by the arm, "Come," he said. "It's time for the service."

Surprised, Jess resisted, gently freeing himself. He had not considered that there would be services happening, though he should have, for Darya had mentioned at breakfast that tonight Jesus would go to the cross and that she and Ivan would take the baby, and possibly Tsura, and they would all be in church for hours. "It will be difficult, of course," she had said, with a small long-suffering shrug that told Jess it was useless to protest.

"Oh, well," he protested now to the priest, "I've got milk in the truck."

"Leave it," the priest said. "It's cold enough out here. It will keep."

Jess was forced to admit he was right. It was cold enough for the milk to keep. Before he knew what was happening, he had followed the priest inside and found himself standing in the back of the church.

Three hours later, he left the chapel, reeling.

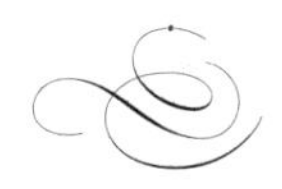

"You can take your milk to the kitchen now," the priest said, stopping Jess as he was crossing the courtyard, already emptied of nuns. "Once that's done, you can come down to the guesthouse, if you like. We are allowed a little wine this evening. Consolation for the Savior's suffering. If you would consent to share a glass with me, perhaps we could talk. I have an idea I would like to put before you. A business proposal, of sorts."

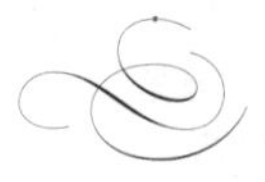

Jess found his way to the kitchen. It was a spacious room with high ceilings and tall doors, no need to duck his head as he wheeled in the cans of milk. Inside, all was clean and quiet, except for a lone nun who was setting a tea tray with small glasses. Next to the tray sat a bottle of clear red wine. The nun reached for it and began to pour the glasses full. He hesitated, uneasy. He had no idea how to speak to a nun, or if he even should. She glanced up.

"You can put the milk in there," she said, and pointed to the pantry where, he could see now, there were several large refrigerators. There was a long counter in that room lined with clean, gallon glass jars. Jess poured the milk off into the jars and moved them to the refrigerators to keep cool. When he came out, the nun had gone.

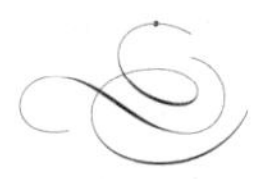

The priest introduced himself as Father Daniel. He was a visiting priest, he explained, down from New York to do the monastery's Holy Week services.

"Are you sure you are a farmer and not a soldier?" he asked, handing Jess a juice tumbler full of a darker, redder wine than the young nun would be serving her sisters about now. "You have just stood through one of the longest and most intense services of the church year."

"To be honest, I didn't want it to end," Jess said. He had a sudden urge to speak freely. It seemed absurd not to, for although before tonight he would have argued against the possibility, he saw that he had found a wider gaze than Pat's. "You see," he went on, "I've recently lost my wife. Tonight, the service, it was so mournful, yet I somehow felt lighter, ached for Gracie less than I have since she died. I've been trying to think why that might be."

"He is a man of sorrows, acquainted with our grief."

"Christ."

"Christ."

"Yes," Jess said quietly, still taking it all in. "I didn't know that before tonight."

Father Daniel peered into his glass. For a moment he was silent. Then he said, "I'm going to tell you something not many people know. I once also had a beloved wife. And while I was in prison for this," he touched his cross, "she was lonely and afraid and took comfort in another man's embrace. I got the news from a guard who knew her lover. Hearing you talk of the ache you feel for your wife, I remember my pain—worse than any beating I received in prison—and I feel compassion for yours. I understand your suffering, or so I think, because I've compared it to mine. But I'll tell you another secret, my friend. This is not true compassion. This is empathy. An emotion which, although very good, comes tainted by all the usual human self-trickery. I believe I care for you when really it is myself I care for most. The proof of this falseness is how soon we weary of empathy when we are required to have it for someone too long. Our stores are limited. Quickly used up. You know this. How long since your wife died?"

"Eight months."

"Eight months. Not yet a year. And only a month, or at the most three, before people stopped asking how you're holding up. If I'm wrong, you may say it."

Jess was silent.

"Yes, well. No surprise. Only Christ, who is pure of even the breath of self-deceit, with no other motive than love, can truly abide our suffering. He accepts to endure it with us indefinitely, never grows uncomfortable or glances away embarrassed from our pain. This is what you felt tonight. The unaccustomed lightness, the joy, if you will, of such a limitless, untiring compassion. You say you didn't know," Father Daniel said, pausing to drink, "but the truth is that like the rest of humanity, you have only forgotten. That is the way of things with Christ. He has long known us. Long loved us. Yet we are always only just getting to know Him."

"Why do it, then?"

"Because we must."

"Yes," Jess said, and sighed. "We must."

He was quiet for a moment, thinking of the light on the mountain all those years ago. He sighed again, rueful. How much he had indeed forgotten. Such a long, longing time it had been.

"There is a prayer we make to Christ," Father Daniel said, his voice growing tenderer, as if he'd heard Jess's thoughts, knew the reason for his sigh. "'Wound my heart with love for you.' Is that not a strange request? It's madness! And yet, don't we understand it, you and me? At least a little. From the moment I saw you, I said to myself, now here's a pilgrim I recognize. A fellow wounded. He has heard tales of a singular healing salve and has been limping about the earth to find out if one truly exists. Tonight, you've made a discovery. Yes, this miraculous ointment does exist. And what is it? More madness! More sweet pain to be endured. More sorrow mingled with joy. It's love."

Here, Father Daniel paused. He gazed intensely at Jess for an instant, his dark eyes lit. Then he said, "You have arrived in Gilead, brother. And I must warn you. This balm burns like fire."

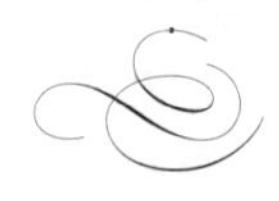

When Jess opened the door at home, he heard Galina fussing. He went upstairs and found her with a sodden diaper, the seat of her pajamas soaked through. Darya came to the door.

"It's all right," he said quietly. "I've got her."

Darya hesitated, her mouth working as if she would protest, but soon she turned and shuffled back down the hall. The bedsprings groaned once, then got quiet.

Jess removed Galina's pajamas, marveling at their small size, and unpinned the wet diaper. On the dresser was a stack of clean diapers, neatly folded. He slipped one under her bottom and fiddled anxiously with it for a while, pinning and repinning. Diapering, it turned out, was not the easy task Darya made it appear. Galina was all belly. She had no more hips than Jess did. But there were no belt loops on a diaper, evidently. After several tries, he pinned it for the last time. Her fussing had grown louder, more fretful. She was out of patience. It was time to admit he lacked the skill to fit it snug. There wasn't a basket or a pail that he could find, so with a guilty glance down the dark hall, he left the wet things in a heap on the floor. He searched the dresser drawer until he found a set of footed pajamas. As he snapped her into them, her cries turned to wails.

"Easy, now," he said. "Easy."

He stroked her soft head, soothing her in the only way he knew how, as he would a horse. She went back to fussing quietly. He carried her down to the living room, sinking with her into his big, deep chair. With her small fat thigh gripped in his hand, her head resting in the crook of his arm, he pulled her close. He crossed his legs, making a nest for her, a position he soon realized, leaning back to test it, suited him too. He had no sooner relaxed, though, and got comfortable when the thought struck him that she might be hungry, and he tensed again. This was something he hadn't considered. He hoped like everything then that she wasn't, for he would be forced to wake Darya, and he didn't want to do that. This baby daughter of his felt good to him, her small warm body nestled against his. He wanted nothing more in the world right now than to just sit with her in this settled-down way. As if she understood, Galina got quiet. She gazed sleepily around, eyelids drooping. Jess bent to her ear.

"Your papa's been in church tonight," he murmured. "What do you think of that?"

The next instant he felt her go limp. She was asleep. With his head resting against the pillowed back of the chair, he closed his own eyes.

What an evening it had been. In his whole life, he had only stepped four times in a church: once to see Rose Marie wed, once to be wed himself, once to bury his wife, and once to see their child baptized. No wonder he had been caught so off guard tonight. He didn't know, even now, what to make of it all. Couldn't fathom what had happened as he'd stood in that dark, smoky chapel with his knees threatening to buckle. Father Daniel, his old back bent to shoulder a massive wooden cross. The gentle lament of the nuns. Lord, that sound alone had been enough to break his heart. It was the light on the peak, and the going of Walter, and the truck plowing over Old Line Bridge, and the muteness of the moon, and the stillborn calf, and Gracie's loving and Gracie's leaving, and the forlorn cries of her baby, and meeting with the sad, strong faces of Darya and Ivan all the livelong day. It was Ivan in the milking shed, blessing the cow. It was wine in a juice tumbler.

It was all that that made him uneasy with Tsura.

It was the eyes in the icon.

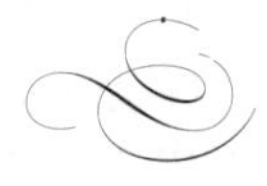

The smell of coffee woke him. When he opened his eyes, he saw that Darya stood next to his chair. The hint of a smile played at the corner of her sober mouth. She held out her arms for the baby, still asleep.

When Jess had finished two cups of coffee, strong and hot and black, he dressed for chores and went outside. There, in the long, thin beam of the barn light, he could see Tsura standing alone on the rise of hill. She was facing east. Jess walked down the hill toward her, toward the sounds of a gently stirring earth, away from the lowing cows and the milking shed. She did not turn as he approached but kept her back to him and her eyes on the dawn. They stood and talked a long while, waiting together for the sun to scale Kerry Mountain and break free of the peak. When at last it did appear in the sky, huge and red and lit with morning fire, Jess was blinded for the briefest moment. By the time his vision had cleared, she was gone.

In the meantime, the cows had grown desperate. They complained now in voices that could not be ignored. Jess turned and went to them, his mind still with Tsura. "It was *her*," she had said, explaining to him in her plain way how she had stood with Gracie in the monastery church, saw in the icon of the Holy Virgin the sad, kind eyes that matched the voice she had heeded all her life. Seeing those eyes and the hands that were full of child, full of God, Tsura understood whose hands it had been that were always held outstretched, ready to help her, quick to save.

And looking at her as she spoke of these things, the hollows of her eyes cast pale and gray in the shadow of the mountain, Jess had seen how tired Tsura was, her patience wearied with longing, and felt his heart align with hers. At long last, he understood.

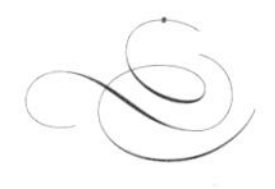

On Ascension Day, Tsura was received as a novice at the monastery. The whole family went out to Mill Bend to commune together and celebrate the feast, even little Galina. Seeing Tsura with the nuns for the first time, Jess had a taste of the bittersweet he knew there must have been in choosing to pledge herself to such a life. She did not look as natural as the others did at prayer, not as she looked sitting cross-legged on the ledge in the spring house, conversing with a toad as with a bosom friend. But it was right. Even a thick-headed fool like him could see it. She wasn't just where she longed to be. She was where she belonged. Her face was as bright as the morning sun.

19

ONE EVENING IN LATE JUNE, in the pink glow before sunset, Jess was unhooking Becky from the plow when he saw an old car rattling its way up the lane. It was a small moss-green coupe, a make and model he didn't recognize. It came closer, and Jess could see the little car was not old at all, only hard used. It did not continue up the drive to the house but turned left at the split in the lane, pulled down by the corral gate, and stopped. Both doors opened at the same time, and a boy and girl got out, merging together as they came around the hood. They linked hands and walked toward Jess.

"Hey," the girl called out.

"Hey," Jess called back, and bent to unbuckle Becky's harness. When he raised his head, he saw that they had come to stand beside him. It was the girl again who said, with a swaying, 1-2-3 cadence to her speech that reminded him of Millie's, "Nice evening. Isn't it?"

"It is that."

"And a handmade sky too."

"Well, now, there I can't agree, not knowing what a handmade sky is."

"My Aunt Zona says when the sky looks like that, Our Lady is piecing a quilt, to lay on the knees of God."

Jess gazed long at the girl, her head tilted heavenward, and then at the sky. He saw that it had turned a deep rose, cut horizontally with slender blue strips of darkness.

"I don't doubt it," he said.

"We heard at the delicatessen in town that you sell fresh cow's milk," the boy said, in an accent that told Jess he was well to the south and west of home. New Hampshire, maybe. Or Connecticut.

"You heard partly right," Jess said. "I used to sell milk to the Amish for cheese."

"And now you don't?"

"And now I don't."

"Well, would you consider selling us a gallon anyway?"

"I might."

"If you did, what would be the price of it?"

Jess thought that was a good question and showed a lick of sense. For from what he could see, any amount he named would be more than they could afford.

Freed from her harness and collar, Becky quivered head to tail, then sneezed the field dust from her nostrils in a thick wet spray. The boy let go of the girl's hand and stepped back. Jess grinned and slung the harness over his shoulder. He slapped Becky on the rump, and she walked off toward the barn. He took up the collar and followed. After a few steps, he stopped and looked back at the couple. They stood in the same spot, hands linked again, watching.

When Jess entered the barn, Becky was already waiting in her stall. He set the tack down against the outside wall, fed her three flakes of hay, and as an afterthought, a can of oats, because he had worked her pretty hard. Ivan's big Hampshire sow, housed temporarily in the stall next to Becky's, heard the sound of feeding going on and rose heavily to her feet, grunting quietly. Hearing the sow, the lambs in the stall adjacent began to bleat. Raising their own meat, and selling the dairy's milk to the nuns, as Father Daniel proposed, were parts of the plan Ivan and Darya had helped Jess make to bring the farm to self-sufficiency. The sow was in pig. She would be moved in the morning to the new farrowing pen. Jess wiped down the collar and harness with a rag, took them into the tack room, and hung them on the wall. When he came out again, the couple was standing in the barn alley.

She was tall and slender, her skin the dark, glossy brown of a husked chestnut. An orange turban covered her hair. He was fair, with a broad, freckled face. Twists of light-red hair fell across the collar of his many-colored coat. She wore only a long sweater against the chill air and had sandals on her feet. The tips of her toes peeped out from the hem of her skirt.

A swallow dipped into the barn then, skimmed over their heads, and landed in the rafters.

"Did you see that?" the girl said in her voice like a waltz. "I felt the wind under its wings as it flew over."

"What kind of bird is it?" the boy asked.

"It's a barn swallow," Jess said. "There's a pair of them up there, working on a nest. I've been luring the cats up to the house all week, feeding them liver paste from a can, to give the birds a fighting chance."

He gazed soberly at the boy and girl, feeling a hundred years old. He could see now that he had misjudged them by firelight. Children indeed. Weary, footsore children, tending a love no more rooted than a new green slip. He saw, too, though, that there was hope in their eyes.

"They mate for life, you know," he said, nodding to the rafters, toward the swallow's nest.

He turned away, then, and headed for the milk room. Somewhere in there, way up high on a shelf, he had seen a gallon milk can with a handle and a lid.

ACKNOWLEDGMENTS

Many thanks to those of my friends and family who read drafts, offered criticism, and generally cheered me on. Would that I had pages enough here to name you all. Special thanks to Judy Lewis for early editing; to my gracious Goodreads friend Mimi, my first unbiased reader; and to Mary Michal White, whose stamina for reading drafts is nothing short of incredible, and whose ability to lift and encourage a flagging heart is one of the great undeserved blessings of my life. Thanks to Jon Sweeney and the staff at Paraclete Press who, while still turning my manuscript into a book with kindness, patience and skill, also got word of it out to readers, without whom a story is "only marks on a page."

Although I've lived most of my life in rural areas and spent my formative years on a 365-acre farm, where our small herd of cows got milked twice a day by hand, childhood memories are too distant to supply the details needed for a story like *Lights on the Mountain*—credit for those goes to my father, Robert E. Taylor. (For errors, the credit is mine.) Many thanks to Billings and Associates, who sponsor the Descansa Percherons of Ash Grove, Missouri, for sharing their knowledge of working draft horses and allowing me to meet the horses at Jade Hills Farms and observe them up close. I'm grateful to Natalia Forni and Tatiana Tildus for advising me on the story's Russian aspects, to Father Alexii Altschul of Holy Archangels Monastery in Weatherby, MO, and to Rev. Mother Magdalena of the Orthodox Monastery of the Transfiguration in Ellwood City, PA for advice on story details of a spiritual nature. (Again, all errors are mine.)

Heartfelt thanks to my brother, Robert D. Taylor, for his tireless efforts to turn a recluse writer into a public author. Thanks be to God for my father in Christ, V. Reverend Father Moses Berry, whose gift of undiscriminating love is rare in this world, to say the least, and gives me hope for heaven. Finally, thank you to my husband Kevin, and to my children Levi and Catherine, who as craftsmen and artists, and as people, inspire me to ask ever more of myself as a writer and as a person.

ABOUT PARACLETE PRESS

Who We Are

As the publishing arm of the Community of Jesus, Paraclete Press presents a full expression of Christian belief and practice—from Catholic to Evangelical, from Protestant to Orthodox, reflecting the ecumenical charism of the Community and its dedication to sacred music, the fine arts, and the written word. We publish books, recordings, sheet music, and video/DVDs that nourish the vibrant life of the church and its people.

What We Are Doing

Books

Paraclete Press Books show the richness and depth of what it means to be Christian. While Benedictine spirituality is at the heart of who we are and all that we do, our books reflect the Christian experience across many cultures, time periods, and houses of worship.

We have many series, including Paraclete Essentials; Paraclete Fiction; Paraclete Poetry; Paraclete Giants; and for children and adults, *All God's Creatures*, books about animals and faith; and *San Damiano Books*, focusing on Franciscan spirituality. Others include *Voices from the Monastery* (men and women monastics writing about living a spiritual life today), *Active Prayer*, and new for young readers: *The Pope's Cat*. We also specialize in gift books for children on the occasions of Baptism and First Communion, as well as other important times in a child's life, and books that bring creativity and liveliness to any adult spiritual life.

The Mount Tabor Books series focuses on the arts and literature as well as liturgical worship and spirituality; it was created in conjunction with the Mount Tabor Ecumenical Centre for Art and Spirituality in Barga, Italy.

Music

The Paraclete Recordings label represents the internationally acclaimed choir *Gloriæ Dei Cantores*, the *Gloriæ Dei Cantores Schola*, and the other instrumental artists of the *Arts Empowering Life Foundation*.

Paraclete Press is the exclusive North American distributor for the Gregorian chant recordings from St. Peter's Abbey in Solesmes, France. Paraclete also carries all of the Solesmes chant publications for Mass and the Divine Office, as well as their academic research publications.

In addition, Paraclete Press Sheet Music publishes the work of today's finest composers of sacred choral music, annually reviewing over 1,000 works and releasing between 40 and 60 works for both choir and organ.

Video

Our video/DVDs offer spiritual help, healing, and biblical guidance for a broad range of life issues including grief and loss, marriage, forgiveness, facing death, understanding suicide, bullying, addictions, Alzheimer's, and Christian formation.

You may also be interested in...

Can You See Anything Now?

Katherine James

ISBN 978-1-61261-931-6 | $16.99

A powerful debut novel that explores grace in the midst of tragedy, and in the lives of unforgettable, utterly ruined characters in the small town of Trinity: suicidal painter Margie; her neighbor Etta; her husband, Nick, the town therapist; their college-aged daughter, Noel, and her roommate, Pixie.

"Brimming with acuity and grace . . . a welcome challenge to the dogmatic conventions of modern Christian fiction." —*Foreword Reviews*

Unveiling

Suzanne M. Wolfe

ISBN 978-1-64060-062-1 | $16.99

Rachel Piers seizes the opportunity to restore a mysterious medieval painting in a church in Rome, leaving behind a bitter divorce and a painful childhood incident. As she restores the damaged artwork, Rachel uncovers layers of her own soul, revealing a courageous woman who comes to terms with a tragic past.

"A quiet, subtle love story deeply grounded in the restoration of art—and human beings." —*Booklist,* starred review

This Heavy Silence

Nicole Mazzarella

ISBN 978-1-55725-508-2 | $17.99

Strong, resilient, and deeply loyal, Dottie Connell farms her family's three hundred acres in rural Ohio alone, having sacrificed love and family for land she does not own. A sudden, inexplicable event forces her to face the past she has worked fifteen years to forget. This beautifully observed novel leads us to question our ideas about motherhood, faith, and the debts we owe.

"Highly recommended."—*Library Journal,* starred review

Available at bookstores
Paraclete Press | 1-800-451-5006
www.paracletepress.com